# Shooting Star
# A Nikki Latrelle Mystery
# Book 5

## Sasscer Hill

## a misterio press publication

---

1. *https://misteriopress.com*

**Also by Sasscer Hill**
***The Fia McKee Mysteries***
*Flamingo Road*
*The Dark Side of Town*
***The Nikki Latrelle Racing Mysteries***
*Racing from Evil*
*Full Mortality*
*Racing from Death*
*The Sea Horse Trade*
***The Quinn O'Neill Mysteries***
*Travels of Quinn*

# 1

The movie camera's dark eye unnerved me. Like a hungry bird of prey, it swept after me as I raced the horse down Santa Anita's backstretch.

Knowing the camera, a Panavision Genesis, recorded my every move and facial expression intimidated the hell out of me. So did the truck and crew rolling dangerously close to our side.

Maybe movie stars like Tom Cruise, who loved to do his own stunt work, get used to this stuff. But me, I was glad I was only an extra, used by the director of photography, or DP, to work out his blueprint for shooting scenes in *The Final Furlong*, a horse racing movie about to be filmed at Santa Anita Park.

Somebody in the truck yelled, "Cut!" The vehicle fell back, and I stood in the stirrups and eased my horse, Daisy Dan. It was the third time we'd shot this scene, and Daisy Dan was tired. The DP, Gabriel Dubois, might be French, stylish, and handsome, but he didn't know a horse from a hamster.

"Okay, Nikki," Gabriel yelled, "that's a wrap. You can take the horse back."

I sketched a wave and patted the horse's sweaty neck, relieved he was done for the day. As I held him to a slow jog, he rounded the far turn of the mile-long oval, before I pointed him toward the gap that would lead us off the track.

The GMC camera truck sped past us, with Dave, the assistant cameraman at the wheel. The pickup had a crane bolted to its bed. It held the Genesis camera, remotely controlled by Gabriel from the passenger seat.

Dave stopped to let Gabriel out by the grandstand. He was probably going to see his contact at Santa Anita's special projects office. As Gabriel walked away, Dave circled the vehicle back toward me. Glancing at his profile, he once again struck me as a nervous loner with secrets to hide. He wasn't the friendliest guy in the movie crew.

Keeping Daisy Dan to a walk, we passed through the gap in the rail, soon leaving the dirt path behind and stepping onto the dirt and gravel of the parking lot. Nearby, Dave rolled in, heading for the base camp, a parking area track management had allotted the studio. The dozen or so trailers for actors, wardrobe, makeup, catering, and camera crew had turned this space into a luxury trailer park.

The air was clear and cool, a dry seventy degrees in February in Arcadia, California. In the distance, the Santa Gabriel mountains rose to meet the golden-blue skyline. No wonder so many people loved living in this state. Except the Arcadia summers were hot and dry, and when the wind blew off the mountains, the forest fires started. I wouldn't want to be around then.

I rode toward the private gate that allowed us into the limited stable area we'd been given. Nearby, Dave paralleled my path, heading his truck for his parking spot by the trailers.

It was late afternoon, and my scene was the last of the day. Most of the movie people had left or were in their trailers behind closed doors and curtains.

Since it was a "dark," or non-racing day, the backstretch was quiet. Grooms would reappear closer to five p.m. to give the horses their evening feed, water, and hay. Now, the area was all but deserted. Sensing a change in the air, I glanced at the mountains. A gray cloud bank had built behind them, and its gloomy presence crept toward me and Dave, who'd parked about a hundred yards away.

A muffled, but sharp pop zinged past me. My gaze swept to the sound of shattering glass. Dave in the camera truck. Blood blossoming from the side of his head.

Horrified, I stared as red gore splattered and spread across the inside of the passenger window. Dave's form slumped and slid sideways toward the passenger door, finally disappearing from my sight.

I knew what I'd seen but couldn't believe it. I forced myself to breathe slowly. Once my nerves steadied to where I could think, I pulled Daisy Dan to a stop, whipped out my phone, and tried to hit a speed dial connection. My hands shook so badly, it took two attempts.

My boss and former fellow jockey, Will Marshall, answered on the first ring.

"Yeah, Nikki, what's up?"

"The cameraman, Dave, was just shot. I think he's dead!" Beneath me, my horse shifted uneasily as my emotions traveled through the reins like electricity.

"Where are you?"

I told him.

"Be there in two minutes."

"This is so bizarre," I gasped. "I'll– I'll call the cops and track security." By now, my horse was alternately backing up lifting both front legs in little half rears. I had to get him moving forward before he exploded. Gathering my reins, I booted him toward the gate and tried to still my trembling hands.

Twenty minutes later, I stood at the murder site next to Will. Around us, the scene was mobbed with police and emergency services. The report of gunfire had brought two fire trucks. They'd flashed in, big, bright and red, with sirens screaming. They were parked now, but their diesel engines still idled noisily.

The dozens of green, wooden barns on Santa Anita's backstretch were flammable enough. The stalls filled with wood shavings and straw bedding were a pyromaniac's delight. Even though we didn't need the fire brigade, I was glad they'd come. Better safe than sorry.

A crowd of gawkers had formed, and cops were all over the place, along with the medical examiner, crime scene investigators, and the ambulance to take Dave's body away.

Two medics wheeled a gurney with what was left of Dave zipped in a black body bag. I had to look away. He might not have been my favorite person but what had driven someone to *murder* him? What could he have done to deserve this?

Mentally I tried to shut out my surroundings and glanced at Will. Now that he wasn't riding, he'd gained a few pounds, and they hadn't hurt his looks. In the past, constant dieting to maintain jockey weight had given his face a honed, almost aesthetic look, enhanced by intense green eyes. When I'd first met him, I'd thought him quiet and a bit introverted until I discovered his wicked sense of humor, part of why I'd fallen for him.

He caught my eye. "You've been here what, four days? And we've already had a murder? What is it about you Nikki? Trouble *loves* you." He managed to keep a straight face, but his lips compressed a little with the effort.

"It's not funny," I protested.

"Sorry, you're right. But it's so typical of what happens when you're around." By now his eyes were bright with amusement and he'd lost his fight not to grin.

I knew Will so well. We'd both seen our share of murder victims and I didn't blame him for seeking refuge in humor.

For a time, we'd been an item. When I was twenty-three, Will was the first man I ever slept with. The relationship hadn't survived. I'd never gotten over how he'd hidden his part-time undercover work from me.

He'd been a subcontractor to the Thoroughbred Racing Protective Bureau when I'd been involved with some bad people at Florida's Gulfstream Park. He'd spied on me, using me to get information back to the Thoroughbred Racing, or TRPB and the DEA. Hard to be certain if he'd come after me as a woman he was falling in love with, one he initially believed was a criminal, or simply a commodity he could use to further his ambition to become an agent for the TRPB.

He'd realized his goal and secured the job. Now, for a short while, I was a subcontractor for the bureau, like he'd been four years earlier. I guess what goes around comes around.

We shared a lot of history and remained friends who respected each other. He'd gotten me the job working for Estrella Studio's movie as an exercise rider and occasional jockey for the race scenes they'd be shooting.

Just then, a man I suspected was a homicide detective for the Arcadia PD peeled away from a group of cops and first responders and headed for us. He looked like so many cops. A cheap suit and hard eyes.

Glancing at Will, he said, "Are you the TRPB agent?"

When Will said he was, the cop thrust out a hand. "Detective Ernesto Garcia." Glancing at me, he said, "Could you excuse us, Miss?"

"Sure," I said, turning on my heel and heading for our backstretch gate. Though I'd turned Daisy Dan over to a groom, I wanted to go back and check on him. I needed to know he was cooling out okay, getting his legs done up properly, and that he seemed comfortable.

The entire string of *Final Furlong* racehorses were older Thoroughbreds. Some of the ones the film company had collected had been running as cheap claimers. As for the rest, who knew where they'd come from or if the movie could succeed at convincing an audience they were top notch racehorses.

One of my undercover jobs was to keep Will informed of the condition and treatment of these animals. Since the mission of the TRPB is to protect the integrity and image of American horseracing, the bureau wanted to avoid the kind of troubles that occurred with the ill-fated HBO racing series, *Luck*. The show had been cancelled after public outcry due to the deaths of several horses on their set.

Since Will wasn't undercover, and I was, I should avoid the appearance of working *with* him. I could be his friend, as long as no one thought I was feeding him information. Remembering the crowd at the murder scene, I wasn't worried about the short time I'd stood next to him. But I'd be careful in the future. My job might depend on it.

Santa Anita management had made it clear to the movie's Panamanian director, Frank Zalaya, that all cast and crew must stay inside the temporary fence surrounding our area. We'd been given a nice thirty-stall barn with wide dirt paths edged with evergreens. I liked the weeping Australian willows and especially the silver-green eucalyptus trees with their fresh, citrus sent. We were forbidden to go beyond the fence. There were too many star trainers at Santa Anita, like Bob Baffert, who'd be very unhappy to have a bunch of ignorant movie people near their barns and horses.

I walked past the Australian willow tree, that along with the movie's security guard, stood sentry by our gate. By now the guy recognized me, and I strode past without having to show ID. Following the dirt path into the backside, I passed beneath a queen palm before stepping onto our shedrow.

Stan Gabrino, the washed-up trainer the production company had hired to manage the horses, stopped me.

"What the hell's going on out there?"

When I told him, I wasn't surprised at his reaction. A quiet sigh and an increased droop in his shoulders were his only comment. Somewhere in his late sixties or early seventies, his wrinkled face and tired eyes were crowned with wispy gray hair.

"Did our string behave themselves today?"

He was referring to the horses. "Yeah, but they pushed Daisy Dan too hard and too long."

With another sigh, he stepped away from me. Sadly, his most prominent feature was a bad limp where his leg had been broken and crushed by a runaway horse. I suspected he desperately needed the job he'd been given and would simply go along to get along.

"Okay, then, Nikki. I'll see you in the morning."

He turned away and hobbled down the shedrow. The guy was useless. Maybe the production company wanted him like that. Turning away from his receding figure, I called to Orlando, who was walking Daisy Dan.

"Hey, how's he doing?"

Orlando shrugged. "He tired. And *el director de fotografía*? He not know what he doing."

"That's why he's the director," I said.

When Orlando led the horse past me, his double gold earrings sparkled, and his teeth flashed white beneath his long, carefully groomed moustache. "*Exactamente!*"

We grinned, and Orlando led Daisy Dan down the aisle before disappearing around the corner of the barn. I'd met Orlando four years earlier when I'd been at Gulfstream Park racetrack. He was a competent groom and I was glad we'd been able to hire him back for this job.

But when things got rough, it was Will I'd trust to watch my back. Orlando, though a cocky little rooster, would run shrieking to the hen house at the first sign of trouble.

But we probably wouldn't have any more trouble, right?

# 2

About an hour later, after giving my statement to Detective Garcia, I climbed into my Toyota parked on the edge of the base camp. Fortunately, the police had placed their yellow crime scene tape beyond my parking spot and hadn't corralled my car.

After firing the engine, I left the track, hung a left on Santa Clara Street and drove to one of those extended stay hotels. The Estrella Studio had rented a block of rooms and given me one. Not fancy, but clean with a decent bed and no bugs. At least not that I could see.

The movie's four stars were arriving the next day, and I'd heard they had luxury suites at Arcadia's Marriott. They'd get the great beds, comfy pillows, nice bathrooms and excellent coffee.

Gabriel had told me that Millie Mason, a well-known, seasoned actress was playing the part of the racehorse owner. She'd started out as a big hit on one of the network soap operas, then graduated to full length films.

Dexter Reddinger, a Texan who starred in a popular modern western series, had the lead male role, playing the part of Millie's racehorse trainer. I liked his series and watched it almost every week. He was attractive, sixty-something, with longish silver hair, moustache, beard and piercing blue eyes. He sat his horse well on TV and should have no trouble riding the track "pony" in the movie.

I'd heard a young, unknown actress from somewhere in Central America would play the lead female jockey. Her name was Catalina Espinosa and apparently, she'd been plucked off a racetrack in Mexico City called *Hipódromo de Las Américas*. Supposedly she'd ridden there as a jockey.

Continuing to muse about the movie and actors, I rolled into the hotel's parking lot, cut the engine, and entered the lobby. A wall-mounted TV was playing a rerun of one of the NCIS shows. A young male star was racing his muscle car after the bad guys. This reminded me of the most interesting addition to *The Final Furlong*.

Jamie Jackson, the hot and handsome twenty-four-year-old English actor, who was all the rage in Britain, was ready to make his US debut. In *our* movie. I was looking forward to getting a look at this guy who was also an ex-steeple chase jockey. At least he'd know how to ride.

I stepped into the elevator and rode to my room on the third floor where I had a great view of the rear parking lot and the back wall of a movie theatre lined with dumpsters. The theatre was part of a strip mall that faced the road paralleling Santa Clara Street.

I took off my paddock boots, stripped my clothes and had a quick shower and shampoo. I'd left my dark hair the way my friend Carla had persuaded me to wear it a few years back. Short and spiky with tendrils at the neck.

I sat in my room's desk chair and fired up my laptop but was soon lost in thought about Carla who'd died tragically four years earlier, and my beloved mentor, Jim Ravinsky, who'd recently lost his battle with pancreatic cancer.

There'd been some hard times since I'd last worked with Will. A relative of a man I'd had trouble with at Gulf Stream Park had claimed ownership of beautiful stallion Diablo, and I'd sold my mare Hellish to a farm in Kentucky that wanted to breed her. Worst of all, I'd suffered a bad fall at Laurel Racetrack two years earlier. Flying down the backstretch on an icy January day, the horse ahead of me had broken down and fallen in our path. My horse had flipped over him, and I woke up in the hospital with a broken collar bone, a fractured pelvis, and a broken leg.

Fortunately, my horse had recovered to race another day. Miraculously I'd escaped spine and nerve damage, injuries that jockeys fear almost as much as death.

Jim had sent me to a trainer friend of his in Aiken, South Carolina, where I'd slowly recovered and finally started exercising the guy's older, seasoned horses. When I'd gotten up to speed, I'd returned to Maryland only to find Jim dying of cancer. Because of my earlier accident I was afraid to ride races, and when Jim got sick, his owners had shipped their horses to other trainers.

*Let it go, Nikki.*

Grabbing the hotel phone, I dialed Will's room. When he answered, I said, "Hey, you want to have dinner or something?"

"Where and when?"

"I don't know. You decide."

"Nikki, what's up? You sound like you lost your best friend."

"I'm fine." I'm also a liar.

"Listen, Nik, cheer up. We've got a movie to make. The stars arrive tomorrow, and we get a lot of nice perks from the studio."

"Like murder?"

"Will you forget about that? I'll pick you up at six."

Like I could forget seeing Dave's head explode inside his truck? That wasn't likely to happen any time soon.

Walking to the kitchen area of my room, I pulled my bottle of Wild Turkey 101 from the cabinet, rattled some ice into a glass, and poured myself a pre-dinner drink. Bourbon doesn't fix anything, but it has a way of making things more tolerable.

I dreamed of death that night and was relieved when the morning sun found its way through the gap in the motel 's curtains. Using my room's coffeemaker, I made a strong cup and swallowed some blueberry yogurt but was unable to banish thoughts of the previous day's carnage.

After slipping into pants and jodhpur boots, I pulled a black turtleneck over my head, grabbed my keys, and headed for the track.

Santa Anita management didn't allow our group to ride out until after regular training hours. The track opened for training every morning from six to ten. They had asked that our horses not show up until the last Santa Anita horse was off the track and the maintenance crew had a chance to do some harrowing.

This put me, the other *Final Furlong* riders, and the camera trucks and crew out there around 10:30 or 11:00, usually from Monday through Thursday, those being dark days.

As I parked my car on the edge of *Furlong's* base camp, I thought about what I'd heard from Gabriel. He and the movie's director, Zalaya, planned to shoot track scenes until dark. This worried me. Did they think they could run horses around the track all day?

Will, who didn't like the idea either, was waiting for me on our shedrow. Our three grooms had already fed the horses, and I was pleased to see them with their heads out of their stalls munching on hay. At the moment, they were happy horses. I hoped it would last.

"I think the red carpet just landed," Will said.

Turning back toward our gate, I saw seven or eight people walking past the Australian willow toward us. Guys in dark uniforms with earbuds were obviously security. The stars displayed designer sunglasses, expertly styled hair, and pricey clothes.

"Remember," Will said, "no photos, ever, or you're out."

When I first agreed to do the job, I'd had to sign all kinds of non-disclosure forms. Today, since the stars were arriving, I'd left my cellphone in my car so it wouldn't be confiscated. These people were so paranoid and secretive about their movie you'd think they were working on the first atomic bomb.

Scanning the group, I thought our DP, Gabriel, was looking particularly French and artistic today with his long dark hair swept back and a big video camera on his shoulder.

The Panamanian director, Zalaya, who I hadn't met before, reminded me of a Latino thug, with his olive brown skin and greased back hair. He wore a soul patch and a scruffy chin beard, that made me want to fire up an electric razor. His snappy, tan safari outfit failed to ease my impression.

Studying the rest of the group, I spotted a young woman with a great figure, and a middle-aged woman with an equally great figure. Their faces were hidden behind large sunglasses, but I assumed the young one was Catalina, and the older, Millie, the soap star. Catalina had luxuriant dark hair to her shoulders, streaked with auburn. The silver hair of Dexter Reddinger was unmistakable, and I felt a thrill of excitement to see one of my favorite stars in the flesh. So much so, that at first, I didn't notice the person behind him.

Gabriel led the group onto our shedrow and made introductions. Hands were shaken, but the newcomers' eyes remained behind walls of tinted glass, until Jamie Jackson removed his shades and extended his hand.

Moving into my space, he took my hand in a firm grip and looked me up and down. "You're the jockey, right?"

"She is," Will said, edging closer.

One of the security guards watched me carefully, then stepped in so close, I thought he might push his way between me and Jamie.

Ignoring the guard, Jamie smiled. "Cat got your tongue?"

Damn him. He *knew* his sexuality was intoxicating. I pulled my hand away, trying not to stare. He looked even younger than 23, like one of those boys you dream about when you're a teenager. The feelings he stirred made me feel like a cradle robber.

He had a beautiful voice. I wanted to hear it again. His skillfully cut hair was long, streaked with shades of blond and light brown, a perfect complement for blue eyes and the kind of long lashes usually reserved for young boys. Wide shoulders, narrow hips and long muscular legs wrapped in tight jeans dissolved any illusions of childhood.

He was trouble, the last thing I needed, but probably not the last thing I wanted.

# 3

When Will led the movie entourage away for a tour of our barn, I was relieved to see the back of Jamie, until I realized I was staring hard at what might be the cutest butt in the State of California.

Orlando appeared at my side, bringing the pungent scent of the liniment he'd rubbed into the horses' legs. He carried a tack box filled with hoof picks, brushes, hoof polish and other tools of his trade.

I was still staring at the receding figure of Jamie, and Orlando's gaze followed mine.

"You know I love *las chicas*, *sí*? I no homosexual, but for that *hombre*?" He finished with a classic Latin shrug.

"I think you're out of luck, Orlando. He likes women."

"He like *you*. I see him looking."

I felt heat rise to my cheeks. "Whatever. We need to get the first horses ready. They've almost finished harrowing the track."

"*Sí, pero,* Catalina, she ride today? *Ella es muy bonita!*"

"She is, but how do you know she doesn't prefer women?"

Orlando threw his hands up. "When you become so *cínico*?"

When *had* I become so cynical?

"Sorry, Orlando. Seeing that guy die yesterday–it really shook me.

He shrugged. "No *problema.*"

"Anyway," I said, "Stan told me that Catalina and Jamie need to settle in. It'll be tomorrow before they ride."

"So, what horses today?"

"Stan should have marked the chart. I'll look."

I walked to the end of our shedrow and into Stan's office. He wasn't there, but a half-empty bottle of Crown Royal stood on a scarred wooden desk. On the wall chart behind it, he'd marked out six sets he wanted ridden that day. He'd also scrawled, "No filming today, just training."

He'd named three for the first set: Predator, Gazelle, and Handsome Henry.

Predator, a dark, almost black bay, with one white sock, had an easy-going personality that belied his name.

The chestnut Gazelle, on the other hand, despite her sweet, doe-like face, was skittish and prone to spooking when you least expected it. She'd also bite you if you weren't looking.

Handsome Henry just wasn't. When no one was around, Will and I called him Crow Bait. The poor guy looked like he'd been picked up off a kill lot.

When I'd encouraged Stan to purchase some body building supplements, treat the horse for ulcers, and fix his teeth, he'd said, "Nikki, you have no idea how cheap these movie people are. They'll pay fifty thousand on air fare and hotels for a star. For everyone else, they spend as little as possible."

"Can't we do something?" I'd asked.

"Let it go, Nikki. It's not our job."

At the tack shop the next day, I spent my own money on some weight building supplements for the horse. Then, I'd cajoled a track vet who was good with teeth into filing down the sharp points on Crow Bait's molars.

That night the horse had cleaned up his feed for the first time. It no longer hurt to eat.

Voices turned me to our entrance gate. Two exercise riders were trying to get past the *Final Furlong* security guard. I trotted over.

"They're okay," I said. "They're scheduled to ride today."

The guard, a tall male who looked like a body builder, compressed his mouth into a stubborn line. "They don't have the right ID."

"They've got their track ID, right?" I said, looking at the two riders. They both nodded. "Look," I said, staring at the guard, "they can't get that ID without a complete background check and fingerprints."

"Sorry, that's not good enough."

"There's not going to be a movie if we can't get these horses out. Can you call someone?"

He frowned and tried to look tough before saying. "Yeah, I could do that." He turned his back, made the call, mumbled something, then spoke to the two riders. "Okay, you can go through."

Knowing I had to work with these movie people, I resisted telling him he was a moron. Instead, I gave him a sweet smile. "Hey thanks, that's great."

A short time later, the horses were tacked up, and we were mounted. Stan had appeared and was giving us instructions.

"Warm them up and two-minute-lick 'em a mile."

The three of us nodded and rode to the track. I'd purposely gotten on Handsome Henry, aka Crow Bait, because I was afraid Stan would ask for too much. No way I was going to whip and drive this horse to run a mile in two minutes. It wasn't racing speed, but it was too fast for his poor condition.

I told the other two riders, Greta and Jerry, to go ahead, then proceeded to jog Handsome Henry for a mile. Trotting around the huge oval, I enjoyed Handsome Henry's horsey scent that grew stronger as he warmed up. I also liked the lemony aroma coming from the silver-green leaves of the eucalyptus trees that dotted the landscape beyond the track's rail.

Greta and Jerry finished well ahead of us, but they stopped, turned their horses back in my direction, and met up with me. The three of us walked back to the barn. As I had expected, Stan was oblivious to the fact I'd ignored his instructions. He was busy getting the next set ready to go out.

After the three of us dismounted and handed the waiting grooms our horses, we climbed aboard three more, and headed back to the track. Stan kept us going through dinner time, and when we finally finished, I went to my room, poured two ounces of bourbon, ordered in Chinese, and collapsed on the bed.

Before I slept that night, I wondered about Catalina. Truth be told, she was too tall to be a jockey. Without a thin-as-a-wire figure she'd never make racing weight. She had lovely full breasts and womanly hips, so it made no sense. I wondered if she was really a jockey and might not be a total miscast for *The Final Furlong*.

"I guess you'll find out in the morning," I mumbled. Burying my face in my pillow, I closed my eyes.

# 4

Greta and Jerry showed up to ride at ten the next morning. I knew they exercised Thoroughbreds for two of Santa Anita's many trainers, and could tell from their dirty boots and dusty clothes they'd been at it for a while.

Though I hadn't needed to, I'd been at the barn since eight. After years of hitting the track at six a.m., coming in later was a luxury I could probably get used to. The thing I couldn't get used to was having real and pretend racehorses at the same track. That was just weird.

Scanning our barn, I saw no sign of Jamie Jackson or Catalina. Probably still lolling about in their plush Marriott beds. But I wasn't their boss and it was none of my business when they showed up. Fortunately, that was the director's problem.

"So, what's happening today?" Greta asked, as I leaned over to pet the stable cat who appeared to have adopted our barn. He arched his back to meet my hand as he padded past my boots.

"We won't know," I responded, "until Stan or somebody from the movie crew gets here."

Greta kept her long blond hair in braids. A few loose tendrils stuck to one of her cheeks. Obviously annoyed, she repeatedly pushed them back. She looked tired enough to quit for the day. She must really need the extra money.

Unlike Greta, Jerry appeared wide awake and ready to go. Sadly, his most distinguishing feature was a face pitted with acne scars. So unfair, because he had a nice nose, good eyes, and would have been handsome.

"So, where are the movie stars?" he asked.

Stan, who'd just limped from his office, gave a dismissive wave of his hand, as if actors, cameras, and directors, were a necessary nuisance.

19

"You're not gonna see them until that French guy gets here."

Jerry's brows rose.

"Gabriel Dubois," I said. "The Director of Photography. He and his crew will be filming us."

"Today?" Jerry asked.

Stan shrugged. "Like I said, we'll know when the French guy gets here. In the meantime, I want you to gallop a few sets to keep them fit enough to look the part."

At that moment, Orlando led Crow Bait from his stall. Greta rolled her eyes and said, "Yeah, right."

Under my breath, I said, "Don't worry, I'll ride him again."

We saddled up and rode out. Greta and Jerry worked their horses into a gallop. When I kept Crow Bait to an easy canter, we fell behind. The sound of galloping hooves and air pumping from the other horses' nostrils faded as Greta and Jerry drew farther away.

I was pleased when at the end of our mile-long canter, Crow Bait was unfazed. Maybe he was tougher than he looked.

When we returned for our third set, we stopped outside the shedrow. Jamie and Catalina, astride Gazelle and Daisy Dan, were blocking the aisle outside the stalls.

When they moved along, Jamie appeared comfortable on the flighty Gazelle, and Catalina seemed to have no problem with the easygoing Daisy Dan. Still, something about the woman rang false.

I stared at her silver-studded leather chaps and spurs. I hoped the wardrobe person, or whoever was responsible, wouldn't put her on other horses with those spurs. They had spiked rowels, for God's sake, and if she used them on a horse like Gazelle, Catalina would find herself in a dust cloud on the horizon.

Greta got an eyeful of Jamie and perked up. "Is that guy fucking cute or what?"

Jerry was looking elsewhere. "That's Catalina, right?" When I nodded, he said, "Those two, right there, are in a dead heat for best looker in California."

So far that morning, I'd only seen Catalina's profile, which did appear sensational. When I'd met the day before, her face had been hidden behind huge sunglasses.

Gabriel arrived in a leather jacket that was as dark and glossy as his carefully groomed hair. After conferring with Stan, he left, probably to join his crew in the new truck they'd brought. I wondered who they'd replaced Dave with. The memory of his brains splattered on the inside of the passenger window caused me to shudder.

Once the two actors gave us enough room, Greta, Jerry and I dismounted and switched to the fresh horses the grooms had readied for us. Orlando gave me a leg up on a big chestnut mare, and we followed behind the actors. The five of us took one turn around the barn before heading for the track.

Once we reached the dirt and gravel parking lot, we fanned out. I wound up next to Catalina, finally getting a look at her face when she turned to speak to me. She couldn't be more than twenty-one. The flawless skin beneath her riding helmet was the color of rich cream with a drop of coffee. Large, almond-shaped brown eyes gazed at me above a straight nose, a wide mouth, and full lips.

She gave me a dazzling smile, revealing perfect white teeth. Like Jamie, she was the full package. They should be hot on the set together.

"So, she said, "they tell me you're a jockey?"

"For about ten years."

"It shows."

I wasn't sure how to take that. Was she saying I looked worn out and washed up, or complimenting me on how I sat the chestnut mare? I suspected the former.

I gave her a noncommittal smile. "And you've been a jockey in Mexico?"

"Yes. A very good one. I've won a lot of big races." Her Latino accent was noticeable, but her English was very good. Certainly, better than my Spanish. But what she'd said sounded like a poorly delivered line off a script, like make believe.

"Have you raced recently?" I asked.

She frowned. "Yes. Why do you ask?"

"You don't look like you'd make racing weight," I said, knowing I was heading into quicksand.

"The requirements in Mexico are more lenient."

"Really. I hadn't heard that." I leaned forward and patted the chestnut's neck, thinking I should disengage. Irritating this woman could get me fired.

She gave me a condescending smile and chose to ignore me. By now, we'd reached the path leading from the lot to the massive Santa Anita dirt oval.

Gabriel stood at the juncture, so we pulled our horses up. Normally, a group of riders wouldn't block the entrance to the track, but we were the only ones out on this non racing day.

The new camera truck stood idling next to the rail. A man I hadn't seen before sat in the driver's seat. I stared at the Genesis camera attached to the front end of the boom. The boom rode on a platform built onto the truck cab's roof. I had no idea how it worked but was interested to see the words "Ultimate Arm" printed on the boom. To me it looked like a crane perched precariously atop the truck's roof.

Will had told me this crane could rotate 360 degrees in less than five seconds and could pan up to 90 degrees a second. It was fully controlled from within the truck and was gyro-stabilized for rough terrain and high-speed scenes like car chases. That was some technology!

As I continued staring, I noticed that a small monitor, behind the camera, faced the truck's windshield. I assumed it allowed the crew to see what was being filmed as they drove forward.

Today the camera pointed ahead. Before, when I'd galloped on the track, it had looked straight at me, like a face.

Gabriel interrupted my thoughts. "Okay, peeps, today we'll be framing a larger group than I did yesterday with Nikki. I want you to gallop down the back stretch bunched up, okay?"

"But I didn't get any sides." Catalina's tone was challenging, her smile suddenly hard. "What, exactly, is my role this morning?"

I wondered what the hell "sides" were, but kept my mouth shut.

"Chill," Jamie said, before turning to Gabriel. "We're not acting today, just practicing for racing scenes, yeah?"

"Exactly," Gabriel said. "There are no sides for today. And I don't want racing speed, just a fast gallop. You got that?"

He gazed pointedly at Catalina, who instead of answering, tightened her lips and tossed her dark hair. Imprisoned beneath her riding helmet, the hair toss lost its effect.

"Yeah, we've got it," Jamie said.

I nodded, Jerry and Greta made noises of assent, and we moved onto the track and booted our horses into a slow jog to warm them up.

It wasn't hard to tell the retired racehorses from what must have been riding horses. My chestnut had been on the track. She took in the view, bowed her neck, and I could see the veins in her neck popping as her blood ticked up. I could also feel her muscles bunching beneath me. I loved that feeling and felt right at home.

Everyone but Catalina looked comfortable. I'd swear she found the huge expanse of track intimidating. It's one thing to be safely confined in a riding ring, quite another to have an endless sea of racing dirt stretching toward the horizon.

Her seat, legs and hands said she knew how to ride, but I had a gut suspicion she'd lied about being a jockey. If my hunch was right, I was glad she was on Daisy Dan, who moved along like an old riding school horse.

When we hit the clubhouse turn, we rolled into a gallop with the camera truck right behind us. We bunched up, Jamie and I abreast on the lead, with the rest on our heels. Jamie grinned at me, then pulled Gazelle close enough to press his knee against mine. I was on the rail with no room.

"Jamie, what the hell are you doing? Trying to put me over the rail?"

"Hardly, luv. I'm enjoying your touch. I like you."

I didn't care how gorgeous he was. I didn't need some movie star hitting on me at a time like this.

"Move over!" I smacked his arm with my crop, leaned closer to the chestnut's mane, and took a cross on her neck with my reins. The chestnut mare read my intention and shot forward.

The truck sped alongside us and Gabriel yelled out the window, "I want you in a bunch, remember? Latrelle, if you can't follow directions, I don't need you here!"

"Sorry," I shouted. "Won't happen again."

"See that it doesn't," he yelled, then the truck fell behind.

Jamie moved toward the center of the track, and I dropped back. He looked at me with a slow smile. "When I first laid eyes on you, I knew you were a wild one."

I gave him my best poker face and looked ahead.

"Okay, luv, I'll behave. Otherwise, you might be filmed committing an assault, yeah?"

He had a gorgeous grin, but I wasn't amused. If the camera hadn't been rolling, I might have given him a rude hand gesture. Instead, I tried to ignore him.

So far, my time in California was going swell. I was stuck with a rogue movie star and an actress playing the role of a jockey, except she'd probably never ridden a race. And somewhere out there was a killer.

# 5

Gabriel insisted on shooting three takes of us galloping in a pack on the backstretch. When we finally were finished, I was pleasantly surprised to find *Final Furlong's* catering company had parked a golf cart at our barn. It was laden with lunch.

Will Marshall, never one to miss a free meal, was eating what appeared to be a grilled Rueben.

After turning our horses over to the grooms, the rest of us crowded around the cart, grabbing sandwiches and plates of fruit and vegetable salads. I bit into a tender beef sandwich that tasted like prime filet. I made a little groan of pleasure.

"Will," I said, "I see what you mean about the perks."

His mouth was too full to answer. I got a wink instead. The two of us drifted away from the others and sat together on a hay bale at the far end of the barn.

I wanted to find out if he'd learned anything about Dave's death. There had to be a reason. Until we knew why he'd been killed, anyone on the set could be in danger. For a while, we were too busy eating to talk.

I noticed Catalina take her plate and walk toward the queen palm. A man I hadn't seen before stood beneath it.

Wiping my mouth with a napkin, I said, "Who's that?"

"Don't know," Will said, standing up to get a better look. "He made it past security, he's wearing a production badge, and Catalina seems to know him. I guess he's okay."

The two appeared to be engaged in an animated conversation. I rose from the hay bale, and taking my empty plate and used napkins, I wandered to the trash bin close to where they stood.

They spoke in rapid Spanish. Catalina sounded upset, and the man seemed to be attempting to calm her. She didn't want to be placated. Her voice rose.

The guy looked about five-foot ten, had light sandy hair, fair skin, and was slender. His suit looked tailormade and he had a large diamond ring on his pinky. It flashed in the sunlight when his hands rose in an appeasing manner.

As I drew closer, they noticed me and immediately became silent. I smiled, said "Hello," and dropped my trash in the bin. When neither one responded, I turned and walked back to Will.

"There's something going on with those two," I said.

"I've met her," Will said. "She's a narcissistic bitch."

I smothered a laugh. "Gee, Will, tell me how you really feel."

He shrugged. "That guy must be with the film company."

"I couldn't tell what they were arguing about," I said. "They were in rapid fire Spanish mode, but it was obvious Catalina was unhappy about something."

"She's probably mad at the studio hairdresser," Will said, "or appalled at by the lipstick they used on her."

He resumed his seat on the hay bale with a chocolate brownie he'd nabbed from the golf cart.

"Forget about her," I said. "Have you learned anything about Dave's death?"

Mouth full of brownie, he held up a wait-a-minute finger. I looked back at Catalina and the well-dressed man. The actress was heading back to the group still gathered around the golf cart, but the man was gone.

Will finished his last bite and took a sip of soda. "I've been in touch with Detective Garcia. Fortunately, the FBI contacted the Arcadia PD for us, and Detective Garcia has agreed to keep the TRPB in the loop."

"Like he had a choice," I said.

I knew that when the TRPB formed in 1946, a guy named Drayton had been made its head. A former FBI agent, he'd been an assistant to Director J. Edgar Hoover, and Hoover had been a big fan of horse racing.

Drayton had modeled the TRPB after the FBI and brought in several agents to work with him. The connection between the two bureaus had remained strong.

Will interrupted my thoughts. "Dave Wells is not who we thought he was."

"You mean he wasn't an assistant cameraman?"

"Oh, he was a cameraman all right. A little too handy with his camera. Turns out, the LAPD has been trying to pin a blackmail rap on him for the last few years. He had a habit of filming people when he wasn't supposed to. He was good at capturing things on film people wanted to keep hidden."

"He had a lot of enemies?"

"No flies on you, Latrelle."

I pictured a long line of people who wanted Dave Wells dead. The thought eased my fear that someone else on the set would be shot.

"So, it might not have anything to do with our film."

Will nodded. "But it's made it harder to narrow a list of suspects. At least they know where the shot was fired. Come on, I'll show you."

We walked beneath the tall palm to the gate, past the drooping willow, and stepped across the lot's gravel and dirt. We passed the base camp before Will stopped and pointed.

"Look toward the back of the grandstand. See the smaller building just before it to the far left?"

I nodded.

"It's used for food storage. Its roof is closer to the ground than anything on top of the grandstand and it's a direct line to the base camp."

"The shooter was on the roof?"

"He was."

I was incredulous. "In broad daylight? Someone would have seen him."

"Someone did. But what they saw was a local roofing contractor's van and a guy in a uniform with a tool kit, climbing to the roof, using a ladder from the van. Apparently, his kit held a sniper's rifle with a silencer, and he was very good at his job. Definitely a professional."

"What about the contracting company?" I asked.

"The van was stolen that morning. The theft was reported, but the killer was in and out of here too fast.

"No prints, no shells?" I asked. "Anything?"

"Nothing of use. Dents in the dirt where the ladder stood, scuff marks on the roof, but no shoe prints. When they found the van, it had been wiped clean."

"Wow." I didn't know what else to say. At least I was a little less afraid of winding up with a bullet in my brain.

# 6

A half hour later, when the caterer's golf cart left the barn, Gabriel called the five riders to gather beneath a silver-green eucalyptus tree.

Waiting for him to speak, I breathed in the tree's citrus scent, and the fresh air drifting down from the Santa Gabriel Mountains in the distance. I could get used to living in California.

"Listen up peeps," Gabriel said. "Normally we'd hire exercise riders from the track to do these practice scenes. You two," he said, looking at Jamie and Catalina, "are costing Estrella a lot of money working these scenes. I could get more exercise riders to come in, and Nikki's always here as she's under contract. But I want to get this right. I need to see how our two stars work together on the track and with the horses."

He combed his hair back with his fingers, then his gaze landed on Catalina. "So, time is money, and I want to film a break from the gate this afternoon."

"Now?" asked Catalina.

"Yes, right now. Everyone game?"

"Bring it on," Jamie said. We all agreed except Catalina. She blinked rapidly before staring at her feet.

When he saw her reaction, Gabriel frowned but didn't comment.

"Orlando", he called, "you grooms get the horses ready."

Orlando displayed his white teeth and gave Gabriel a little salute. I trotted to the groom.

"Who am I scheduled to ride?"

"Mr. Stan, he put you on Mystery Ride."

"Okay, I'll get the horse ready."

28

I'd just as soon put the tack on myself. Especially the girth, if I was breaking from the gate. Both the leather girth and the stretchy over girth had to be snug enough to keep me safe. When a horse busts out of a starting gate, he generates tremendous force. Equipment has been known to break.

I liked Mystery Ride. I'd looked up his stats after I'd first seen him. He'd been a useful racehorse by the excellent sire, Candy Ride. He should play his part well.

"Who are you putting Catalina on?" I asked.

"The grey mare."

"That should be all right. Orlando, see if you can get her to take those spurs off."

"Madre de Dios! I not tell her what to do. You think I loco?"

"I see your point, Orlando. Never mind. I'll say something to Gabriel."

Before putting the tack on Mystery Ride, I walked back to Gabriel. "Mr. Dubois–"

"Gabriel, please," he said.

I smiled. "Sure. Gabriel, I'm worried about those sharp spurs Catalina is wearing. If she rakes the wrong horse with those things, your star could end up in the next county."

"Thank you, Miss Latrelle. But what a star wears comes directly from wardrobe and the film's director, Mr. Zalaya. It is not my job to tell the stars what to wear."

"Couldn't you say something to Zalaya? What she's doing is dangerous."

"I'd rather not," he said. He turned his back on me and left the barn area.

"Your funeral," I muttered. Was Gabriel that intimidated by Zalaya?

I tacked up Mystery Ride, a dark bay gelding with no white markings. There were several horses like that in the barn. Probably, so more than one horse could play the same role. With washable paint, the studio could turn a plain bay into Predator, the horse with one white sock–or any other horse for that matter.

A short time later, we'd warmed the horses up and were standing behind the starting gate as the track's gate crew began loading us. One guy was quick to grab Catalina's reins, no doubt wanting to get close to her. She had reapplied her lipstick, dusted on more blush and looked sensational.

Aboard one of the plain bay horses, she was still wearing her fancy chaps and silver spurs. She had a white-knuckle grip on her reins and beneath the blush, her face had turned pale.

A crew member led me into the gate. Mystery Ride shoved his nose right against the metal that would snap open when the starter released the electric hold on the doors. Mystery Ride was ready.

I leaned forward, took a cross on my reins, grabbed mane with one hand, and waited. Greta was the last to load. Seconds later the bell rang, the metal doors crashed open, and the horses burst out of the gate. In my peripheral vision I saw the front feet of Catalina's horse come back to the ground. It must have reared coming out of the gate. The horse flashed past me with no rider.

Gabriel, on his megaphone, yelled at us to cut the scene. Everyone did the best they could to ease their pace, except me. Since there was no outrider on the track to catch the loose horse, I sent Mystery Ride after him.

It took about an eighth of a mile before I was able to pull alongside the runaway. I leaned forward, grabbed his reins and leaned back with my feet in the stirrups like they were a dashboard. I pulled both horses up. After circling back at a jog, I returned to the gate. The same crew member came and took the reins of Catalina's horse from me.

Shaking his head, he said, "I just told her she might not want to spur the horse when the gate opens this time."

I couldn't help but grin. "Did you suggest she take the spurs off?"

"Yeah, I made that mistake, and she told me to do something unpleasant in Spanish."

"Is she all right?" I asked.

"Yeah, once we dusted her off. She was mad as a wet hen, said it was my fault. Man, she is some piece of work."

And yet he had taken her horse again. He must not be ready to break the spell she'd cast on him. Beautiful people are hard to resist. With that thought, I glanced at Jamie only to find him staring at me.

"Brilliant catch out there, Nikki," he said.

For the first time, I saw respect in his eyes. His hands on the reins looked strong and competent. I imagined those hands on–

Gabriel's megaphone blared from the far side of the gate. "Okay, peeps, let's load up again and do it right this time."

They put me in the gate next to Catalina. She had a death grip on the reins and suddenly I felt sorry for her. For whatever reason, she was out of her depth.

She glanced at me, and I gave her a smile. "Keep those spurs off him and you'll be fine. Just sit on him and let him do the work."

She gave me a tense nod, and we were off again. She stayed with the horse this time, and once we settled into a steady, fast gallop, she seemed to be enjoying the ride. She knew her way around a horse, just not the racetrack.

So, why had Zalaya chosen her for the role of jockey? Could he be sleeping with her? Or was something else going on?

# 7

When we knocked off that evening, I untacked my horse in his stall and handed him over to the groom, Ramon. Stepping outside, I felt a little thrill of surprise to find Jamie leaning against the shedrow's railing, apparently waiting for me.

"Hiya," he said.

"What's up?" For God's sake. Did I have to sound like Bugs Bunny?

He smiled, his teeth as perfect as Catalina's. My internal efforts to label him a plastic movie star weren't working. I'd avoided looking at his eyes, his mouth. Instead, I realized I was staring at his hands again. Strong, hands with long tapered fingers that led me to imagine things better left unimagined.

"You fancy a bite to eat, luv?"

"I don't know," I said. "It's been a long day."

"Tomorrow's Friday. They've got live racing, and we won't be allowed on the track, yeah? Have a drink and a meal, then I'll show you how they're putting together our sound stage."

*That*, I did want to see. I barely knew what a sound stage was, let alone what one looked like. I felt my lips curve in a smile.

"Okay, I'd like that."

"Good. How about I collect you at your hotel an hour from now?"

"You *know* where I'm staying?"

"Girl that looks like you? I had to find out, didn't I?"

I recognized false flattery when I heard it. Still, he was so damned appealing.

"Yeah, okay. I'll see you then."

An hour later, I stood outside my hotel, wearing a new pair of black jeans and a lavender cotton shirt. The upscale manufacturer had added a design of black and turquoise racehorses to the collar and cuffs. I'd fluffed my short hair with mousse and applied lipstick and mascara. While staring at the bathroom's full-length mirror, I'd grinned and saluted my reflection.

A low, but powerful, rumble drew my eyes to a dark metallic-blue convertible. As it rolled up and stopped before me, I made out the brand name, Porsche. Beneath that it said Carrera S.

I admit it. I'm a snoop and had every intention of Googling the car at the first opportunity. I wanted to know how much it cost.

Being a low-slung convertible, it gave me a great view of my dinner date. He was wearing a black suede jacket and a white spread-collar shirt with black jeans and tooled cowboy boots.

Climbing into his car felt a bit like climbing into a spider web.

Jamie saw my expression. "Don't be afraid of the car, luv. I'm a good driver."

"I'm not afraid of the car." Seeing a slow grin spread over his lips, I changed the subject. Waving a hand at the dash and gleaming hood of the Porsche, I said, "You must make an excellent salary in the movie business."

"A hell of a lot more than I did riding chasers in England, but this isn't my car. It's a rental."

"Where do you rent a car like *this?*" I asked.

"In LA, where else?" He laughed, shifted the car into gear and off we went.

Flying along in the convertible, I was thankful my short hair tended not to tangle. Before long, the big engine slowed, and Jamie turned into the lot of a restaurant called The Derby.

Inside, the walls were built from old, rose colored brick, and decorated with racetrack memorabilia. Crisp, white tablecloths covered the wooden tables, and brass chandeliers and small table lamps provided soft lighting.

After being seated at a somewhat private corner table, a waiter handed me a menu. I read the back panel with interest. Legendary jockey, George Woolf, had purchased the restaurant in 1938, when he was at the top of his game and "Sea Biscuit" was a household word.

Reading this I felt a bit nostalgic for my former boss, Jim Ravinsky, and our groom, Mello, both of whom had had a vast knowledge of horseracing lore stored in their heads. My mom, who'd died when I was thirteen, had also been a racing fan.

In Woolf's day, racing had been safe from the competition of football and world soccer cups. Horseracing had dominated public radio and daily news column inches. Lots of inches.

"You're lost in your thoughts," Jamie said. "May I order you a drink, and you tell me about them?"

"See if they have Wild Turkey 101, would you?"

He nodded, signaled the waiter.

The mouthwatering aroma of grilled beef, roasting potatoes, baking bread and a touch of garlic filled the air.

"Hey, I'm still waiting on your thoughts," he said.

"I was just thinking about the glory days of racing, and how popular it was."

"You sound wistful," he said, "I get it. Back in the day there were no wankers like PETA marching about, determined to destroy the sport."

"Exactly," I said, "and the newspapers wrote enthusiastically about racing. Now they pounce on and magnify any negative detail they can dig up."

He studied me a moment. "I like talking with you. The film business has moved me away from the people who understand or care about horseracing."

His increased interest in me made me nervous and giddy. I was relieved when the waiter set our drinks before us. I took a big swig of liquor, immediately felt better, and studied the menu.

The Derby had a terrific beef selection, and I zeroed in on the tournedos of filet mignon, almost whimpering at the description.

*Twin four-ounce filet mignon medallions placed on grilled tomatoes, crowned with our own Béarnaise sauce and topped with mushroom caps.*

By now, I was hunched over the menu, staring at the description like it was a winning lottery ticket.

"You don't get out much, do you, Nikki?"

"Not to places like this," I said. "And don't laugh at me."

"I'm not," he said, though his eyes were bright with amusement. "Look, I had my hard times riding chasers in England. I used to sleep in my car, and I've had my share of dodgy fish and chips." He waved at the ambiance and luxury that surrounded us. "I never ate like this unless I won a big purse, and then I'd blow it all and be half starved by the end of the week."

I knew what that was like and almost told him how after my mom died, I'd been forced to steal food from snack shops and gas station markets. But that had been a long time ago, and he didn't need to know about it.

"Order whatever you want," he said. "I can afford it. Besides you're part of the team, yeah?"

The waiter came, and I ordered the tournedos and another drink, figuring I could handle the booze with the meal that was coming. I relaxed and began to enjoy Jamie's company.

We had more in common than I'd realized. We traded race riding stories and ended laughing ourselves silly. About the time I finished my second drink, he was on a roll, and brought up the hard and hungry times again.

"I tell you luv," he said with a serious expression, "my life was a shambles. Sometimes I drank coffee stains and I'd eat the donut holes, too."

My laugh came out as a little snort, and I could feel the heat of embarrassment rising to my cheeks.

His only comment was to signal the waiter. "I think the lady needs another drink."

"No, thank you," I said.

As the waiter drifted away, I tore into the warm crusty bread and slathered it with butter. I was not going to lose my head with Jamie.

About the time I was digging into my filet, the light-haired man, who'd argued with Catalina, entered the restaurant. Two olive-skinned men with dark hair accompanied him. Like the blondish man, one of the other fellows had a flashy diamond pinky ring, and the third wore a heavy gold linked necklace.

"Jamie, do you know that blond guy who just came in?"

"I saw him once before. He came out of Zalaya's office when I first went to Estrella Studios for my interview. We weren't introduced, so I don't know his name."

"Catalina does," I said. "She was arguing with him during our lunch break today."

"Sorry, luv, I can't help you. But those two with him are a bit dodgy looking, yeah?"

"Maybe the thug look is popular in California," I said. "It's my first time out here, so what do I know?"

"About as much as I do," he said.

The maître d' seated the three men across the room from us. I forgot about them when Jamie began relating his transformation from jockey to movie star. After that, our waiter brought a dessert menu filled with calorie-laden delights.

While we lingered over coffee and chocolate mousse, the three men paid their bill and left.

"They were in and out fast," I said, staring at their retreating figures.

"I don't mind seeing the backs of those last two," Jamie said.

I didn't know why, but I felt the same way.

# 8

When we left The Derby, Jamie held the door of the Porsche open for me. "Now," he said, when I climbed in, "I'll show you the sound stage. It's where most of the acting takes pace."

"I thought it was going to be filmed at the track," I said.

Settling into his bucket seat, he said. "No, that's not how it works. Action scenes with the horses and a scene or two at the barn and in the grandstand is probably all they'll use for the movie."

"What about Dexter Reddinger? Won't he need to be around the barn?"

He fired up the Carrera, and I was thrust back in my seat as we rocketed out of the parking lot.

"Afraid you won't be seeing much of him," Jamie said. "Reddinger and Millie Mason's scenes will mostly be shot on the sound stage. Besides, they're back in Hollywood. Millie is finishing up a film for Hallmark, and Reddinger's probably looking at projects with his agent."

As I listened, we whizzed past fancy replicas of Victorian homes, their gingerbread woodwork painted a crisp white. Palm trees abounded and black wrought iron fences outlined the properties. Passing into an older neighborhood, I saw adobe style homes beneath red tile roofs, surrounded by lush plantings.

"So," he continued, "they'll probably come back as soon as the sound stage is ready. You can expect Reddinger's barn scenes to be limited to a day or two."

"Oh," I said, my voice dampened by disappointment.

"But you'll see a lot of me," he said, an impish grin settling on his face.

Though I gave him a "whatever" shrug, a wave of nervous anticipation shot through me. About twenty minutes later, we reached a large lot that appeared to take up the entire block. The silver gleam of a new chain link fence, topped by razor wire, surrounded the property. Just inside the fence, a wall of evergreen thuja plants blocked our view. I could only see the roof and a snippet of cinderblock walls, giving me the impression of a large warehouse.

"They've done an ace job with this," Jamie said. "Last I was here, there was a rusty, broken down fence and no hedge. They threw serious cash at this project! Be interesting to see what they've done inside."

"I don't think we'll be able to get in," I said, pointing at a closed gate with a guard house behind it.

"That wasn't here last time either." He rolled the Carrera forward, and when its nose almost touched the gate, Jamie climbed out.

The guard house had tinted windows, and I couldn't see inside. Jamie called out, "Hello?"

When he pushed on the gate with his hands, a man stepped out from behind the tinted windows. He was dressed in a security guard's uniform, and I was surprised to see a gun holstered on his hip.

"Step back from the gate," he said, and Jamie did. "This," he continued, "is private property. No admittance. You need to leave."

"Yes, sir, but we work for Estrella Studios. We're cast members, yeah? Just hoping to see how our sound stage is progressing."

"No can do, buddy. You need to leave."

Beyond the gate, I could see a large section of the warehouse's wall. A metal door creaked and swung open. *The Final Furlong's* director, Frank Zalaya emerged. Shading his eyes against the setting sun with one hand, he stared at us.

Zalaya pulled a cellphone from his pocket, and seconds later, the guard's phone rang.

He answered the call, pivoted to look at Zalaya, then turned to gaze at us again. "Yes sir. Of course, sir," he said. Putting his phone away, he spoke to Jamie.

"You're cleared, but you need to give me your cellphones. I'll give 'em back when you leave."

"What's with the cellphones?" I asked, after Jamie handed them over.

"They're farther along than I thought if they're already banning pictures. They don't want photos on social media that identify the studio's location. And

God forbid you photograph them shooting a scene with Dexter Reddinger and put it on Instagram. You'd probably get fired."

"*Why?*" This struck me as absurd.

By now, Jamie had reached the warehouse and was parking the Porsche by the building's door. "Nikki, movie people can be daft when they film a popular series like *Game of Thrones*. They're paranoid and secretive. Afraid an upcoming scene or plot line might leak."

"But that's stupid," I said.

"Not if you consider the money coming from the sponsors. You think they'd be happy if the new episode a million people are waiting to watch is no longer a surprise?"

"Yeah, I see your point."

"Listen, when I worked on a series in England, they gave me a script to study. Then right before the shoot, they gave me my sides." When he saw my blank expression, he said, "That's a piece of script for, say, just one scene. The thing is, what they handed me was different than the original script."

"Better you than me," I said, shaking my head. "I'm glad my contract doesn't include speaking parts."

We walked through the door to find a cavernous room inside. About halfway down it, Zalaya was talking to what appeared to be the boss man for a bunch of carpenters. The men were busy with two by fours, building a stud wall against the cinderblock of the warehouse. Other men were following behind, stuffing insulation into the newly made framework.

Union electricians were on scaffolding running wires in the ceiling. The sharp smell of freshly sawn wood hit my nostrils, followed by a stuffy scent that must be the insulation and sawdust.

"They're soundproofing," Jamie said. "Next, they'll nail sound board overtop, put foam cones on the ceiling, and you won't be able to hear a jet take off in the parking lot.

As we approached Zalaya and his greased back hair, his unusually long and narrow soul patch almost stopped me. It was kind of creepy, like a landing strip for flying parasites.

But the sudden eagerness that lit his face immediately reduced the weird factor, especially when he threw us a bright, welcoming smile. "This baby's right on schedule," he said. "That'll keep them happy."

He seemed more than just happy to be on schedule, he seemed relieved. Like maybe he'd been afraid of something. I was probably overreacting. Besides, what did I know about making a movie? For that matter, why should I judge how this man groomed his whiskers?

Zalaya seemed to vibrate with excitement as he led us to the far end of the warehouse and waved an arm toward the back. "This whole wall will be green screen!"

When I gave Jamie another blank look, he said, "It's for special effects. Suppose I stood before the screen and behind me, they ran a film of a stallion rearing and striking. In the final cut, it would look like I was about to be killed."

"Wouldn't you look like you were stuck on top of the horse scene?"

"Nope. Green is the color most unlike skin tones. Makes us pop and look real."

"But don't wear a green outfit," Zalaya said, grinning. "It'll merge into screen's color, and you'll be a head and hands without a body."

The guy might look like a sleaze bag, but he had a childlike enthusiasm that was infectious, and I liked him for it.

When we finished our tour, Zalaya walked us out to Jamie's car. I could feel the director's sudden anxiety, almost before I saw it on his face. I followed his gaze to an SUV parked about a hundred feet away.

It looked like two men were inside. I couldn't make out their faces, but the sparkle of a diamond at the steering wheel and a flash of gold on the neck of the passenger made me think it might be the two creeps I'd seen at The Derby restaurant.

"Who's that?" I asked.

"Nobody," Zalaya said. "Hey, it's getting late and I got to close up. Maybe you two should hit the road, okay?"

"Sure," Jamie said. "We'll be off, then."

When we climbed into the car, Zalaya disappeared into the warehouse, and Jamie and I exchanged a look.

"Wonder what got into him?" he said.

"Don't look now, but I think those two thugs we saw earlier are in that SUV over there. I think they spooked Zalaya."

Jamie turned his head and stared. "They give *me* a bad feeling, too."

"Then whip up those Porsche ponies and get us out of here," I said.

We grabbed our phones at the guard house, Jamie hit the gas, and moments later we were a rumble in the distance.

# 9

The next morning, Crow Bait, aka Handsome Henry, came up dead lame when I tried to jog him around the shedrow. I climbed off the horse, and Orlando and I stood staring at his left front leg.

"Looks like an old suspensory injury has flared up," I said.

Orlando knelt by the horse and ran his hand down the back of Crow Bait's leg below the knee. "*Sí*, has much heat."

"Look at the profile," I said. "You can see the swelling." I'd encountered worse, and I thought with rest, cold hosing, and poultice, the horse would come around. But only as a riding horse, not for constant galloping on a movie set. Why had Stan even purchased this horse?

"Put him away," I said, "and see if you can get him to stand that leg in a bucket of ice. I'll see what Stan wants to do."

For a man who'd purchased *The Final Furlong's* racehorses and was supposed to oversee them, Stan seemed to do very little beyond what Gabriel told him to do.

As I walked to the trainer's office. a damp breeze kicked up and blew through the shedrow. On the western horizon, a cloud bank was building in dark layers. I'd packed rain gear when Will had said February was Arcadia's wettest month. But each day since my arrival had been sunny, so of course, my raincoat was at the hotel. I hoped the bad weather would hold off.

When I reached Stan's office, he was sitting at his battered wooden desk drinking from a china mug. The acrid smell of burnt coffee emanated from a glass pot on a nearby shelf. A whiff of Crown Royal laced the air as well, and I suspected he'd added a dose of the liquor to his cup.

Only eleven o'clock, and he was drinking whiskey.

"Handsome Henry's lame," I said.

"Good morning to you, too, Nikki."

I wasn't going out of my way to be civil to this guy. "What do you want to do?"

"Get rid of him. He's no use here."

"How do you plan to 'get rid' of him?" Anger flickered in my gut. I'd been in the business long enough to know Crow Bait might be headed for the killers.

"Don't worry about it," he said. "I got a guy that'll come take him."

"And cram him into a double decker truck bound for Mexico?"

Instead of answering, he stared at his coffee mug.

"Look," I said. "Let me take care of it for you, okay?"

He swallowed more coffee. "Knock yourself out. But I want him out of here by tomorrow. I got another horse coming in to replace him."

Not bothering to hide my anger, I said, "So, you already knew he was lame."

"Just get him out of here."

"Yes, sir," I said. "Whatever you say."

I stalked out of his office, and later, after Greta, Jerry and I had finished with the rest of the horses, I called Will.

"We need to talk. Can you meet me for coffee at the Starbucks across from our hotel?"

He agreed, and I found him sitting in an armchair by a table in a rear corner. He had his back to the wall as he watched me walk toward him.

I set my coffee and sandwich on the table and sat opposite him. "You've turned into a real cop, Will, haven't you? Got your back to the wall in case some armed felons rush the joint?"

"Don't make fun, Nikki. A guy was murdered, remember?"

Like I'd ever forget *that* day. "If I was making light of things, it's probably because I'm getting worried, okay?"

"Tell me," he said. "You've always had good instincts."

I recounted seeing the guy who'd argued with Catalina and his two companions, and how later, I was pretty sure they'd spooked the hell out of Zalaya.

"Will, do you think they might be connected to Dave's death?"

"Anything's possible. But Detective Garcia is still focusing on people who aren't connected to the movie. He believes it's most likely a blackmail victim who had Dave Wells eliminated."

"Still," I said, "between the way that blond guy was arguing with Catalina and those lowlifes he was with last night, I get a bad feeling. Jamie did too. It would be nice to find out who this guy is."

"I'll find out," he said. His face muscles tightened. "So, are you and Jamie Jackson an item now?"

I'd always had a thing for guys with intense, intelligent eyes like Jamie's, and Will's green ones were high on that list. But my private life was no business of the TRPB's, and none of Will's, either.

"I had dinner with him. That's all. Not that it concerns you, anyway."

"Nikki, I know how you are with younger, bad boys. You get reckless and don't seem to care who you hurt."

He might as well have punched me in the gut. "That was low, Will." I couldn't meet his eyes and stared at the table instead.

He was referring to Bobby Duvayne, a sexual predator who'd mesmerized me and my young friend Lorna at Colonial Downs five years earlier. Lorna had lost her virginity to Bobby and been crazy in love with him. And me? I'd been seconds away from doing the deal with him myself, when I'd come to my senses and stopped. But Lorna had found us together, and I'd lost a good friend.

"I don't pretend to be perfect, Will, and I'll always regret hurting Lorna."

He reached across the table and covered my hand with his. "You're right. That *was* low and I shouldn't have said it. Anyway, don't beat yourself up. That guy would have only hurt Lorna worse if their affair had continued. He was a bad piece of work."

Not wanting to linger in the pain of my past mistakes, I changed the subject. "Listen, Crow Bait is lame, and I need to find a place for him before Stan sends him to the killers. Would the TRPB have a list of horse rescue people?"

"Good idea," he said and pulled out his phone. "There's a guy named Brian. Works computers in TRPB's home office in Fair Hill. An agent I met named Fia said to call Brian when I needed answers."

"But this guy's in Maryland," I said. "We need to find a *local* rescue."

"Nikki. For once, could you have a little patience? Let me make the call and see what happens. The TRPB has long tentacles."

Five minutes later, he'd finished his call. "We're in luck, there's a rescue farm just outside Arcadia."

"That's great," I said. "Give me their number, and I'll take care of it."

As Will wrote down the information and slid the paper across the table, I wondered again why Stan would have purchased a horse like Crow Bait.

"Let me ask you something, Will. Do you think Stan is buying these horses and skimming off the top? I wouldn't be surprised if he took $5,000 from Estrella to buy a horse, paid the seller $4,000, and kept the rest for himself."

"That's the studio's problem," Will said.

"Not if these horses start breaking down, and social media gets wind of one being sent to the killers. How would that make racing look?"

His eyes narrowed and he gave me a sharp look. "You have a point. You'd make a good agent, Nikki."

I rose to leave. "I'd rather stick with the horses. You're the agent. You'll let me know when you find out that guy's name and how he's connected to *The Final Furlong,* right?"

He said he would, and I left.

Outside, a cold, wet wind hit me. Rain began pelting down in sheets. As I ran toward the hotel, the cloud bank closed in and it grew dark. The weather blew my thoughts back to the two men who'd seemed to frighten Zalaya so much.

They'd unnerved me, too. And suddenly, fear, as hard and cold as the rain, struck me. I couldn't stop thinking that someone besides Crow Bait might be facing a one-way ride to a slaughterhouse.

# 10

Sunday morning, it was still raining when a horse trailer came to pick up Handsome Henry. Thanks to several days of ice, poultice, and Orlando's secret liniment mixture, the gelding was almost walking sound.

The trailer had parked near our private entrance, and as I walked toward it, I saw the words "Pay It Back Rescue" emblazoned on the side.

The woman driver climbed out and followed me through the rain back to the shedrow, where Orlando had Handsome Henry out and ready to go. Handing his lead shank to her, I patted the gelding's neck one last time.

"Listen, Crow Bait, this lady's gonna turn you back into Handsome Henry again, okay?"

Beneath the shelter of the shedrow roof, he leaned his head against my chest, and I scratched him between his ears. It was his sweet spot, and he would have stood there all day if I'd kept rubbing.

"Nikki," Orlando said, "You let him go now. New horse coming. I have to make stall."

I'd forgotten that Stan had already found a replacement. "You know anything about this new horse?" I asked him.

He shook his head and stroked one of his long moustaches. "Nada. Mr. Stan, he no say."

"What else is new?" I said.

I turned to the woman and thanked her for taking Crow Bait. Will and I had reached into our wallets the day before, and I was able to hand her a hundred-dollar donation.

She thanked me and said the rescue farm already had a teenage girl in mind that was looking for a horse. By now, my arm was possessively draped over Crow Bait's neck.

"You know," she said, "I should probably hit the road."

Orlando grinned. "Nikki, she no like to say goodbye."

It was true. I didn't, at least not to horses. I made myself step back and watch as Crow Bait was led away. I wished him luck.

That afternoon, the storm blew off to the east. Silver, blue and gold streaked the sky above the stable yard, where one stall stood empty. As I watched the horses tearing wisps of timothy from their hay nets, I hoped Stan had chosen wisely when selecting Crow Bait's replacement.

Gabriel had arranged a meeting, and I waited for him to arrive with the two exercise riders . Moments later, Jamie and Catalina showed up, and Will followed them. Gabriel bustled in, his long hair plastered back as if he'd been caught in the last of the storm.

It was still quite cool from the rain, and both Gabriel and Jamie wore leather jackets. Catalina had wrapped herself in brown suede and hidden her eyes behind sunglasses.

Finger combing his dark hair, Gabriel spoke. "Listen up, peeps. Tomorrow, we shoot film for real, okay? Jamie, you and Catalina know the drill. If the sides Zalaya gives you tomorrow have changes, you'll handle it, right?"

They both nodded.

"I want everyone here at 9:30 sharp. We ride out as soon as the track is closed for training and harrowed."

I thought we were about to be dismissed, but Zalaya appeared beneath the queen palm. He stopped at the edge of our group, rubbing at his soul patch with two fingers. Then, he broke into a smile.

"The Arcadia sound stage is open for business! The carpenters and electricians cleared out at lunch time. The cameras are ready!"

I was surprised when the two actors and Gabriel burst into applause. After an exchange of glances with Greta and Jerry, we applauded too.

"Thank you," Zalaya said, before taking on a more serious tone. "Jamie, I want you and Catalina there at 7:00 a.m. for your scene with Millie and Reddinger. We'll film the four of you, then Gabriel will bring you over."

He paused a moment. His chin rose, his shoulders straightened, and his gaze settled on Jamie and Catalina. "You people are going to *love* the sound stage. We've built some really cool replicas of the grandstand restaurants and betting parlors."

"So, the stage crew will work with Millie, Reddinger, and the extras. The gambling scenes should be great!"

His eyes narrowed, his focus singling out Catalina. "Be on time tomorrow. We're on a tight schedule." He took a step back. "That's all."

I looked around to see if we should clap like trained seals again. Apparently not, Zalaya had already turned away.

Will moved next to me, and we exchanged a "whatever" shrug. At the sound of wheels, we turned. The catering company's golf cart was rolling in with a bucket of iced champagne and a silver bowl of chocolate-covered strawberries.

Gabriel lifted the bottle and sliced at its neck with a long sharp knife. The cork popped and released a spray of froth and foam that rolled down the bottle's neck.

"*Ooh la la*!" Jamie said. "Did Estrella pony up the money for a bottle of Veuve Clicquot?"

"No," Gabriel said, "They're too cheap. I paid for it. You're my peeps and you will have fine champagne at the beginning and end of this film!"

"Brilliant," Jamie said, as he grabbed a flute from the cart. Gabriel filled the glass with bubbly, and Jamie handed it to *me*.

Catalina's lips tightened into a pout. A glance at Will showed raised brows, so I gave him an impish grin and held my glass in a toast before taking a huge sip. The stuff was delicious.

Jamie must have noticed Catalina's annoyance, since he quickly handed her the next glass. Then, he handed one to Greta, almost knocking her out with his practiced sexy smile. She turned bright pink.

I felt like we were actors playing a role, like we were on the set of a movie. Wait, we *were* on the set of a movie. I hoped the script didn't include Catalina grabbing the champagne knife and plunging it into my heart.

Fortunately, everyone's attention was drawn to Orlando as he came through the entrance gate leading a big, beautiful chestnut horse. The animal's coat was a dark gold red, and his flowing mane and tail were flaxen. A white blaze and four white socks completed this picture of perfection.

"*Ooh la la*," Jamie said again. "That's more like it."

Catalina walked quickly toward the horse. "He's gorgeous. I will ride him!"

"I'll have to discuss that with Stan," Gabriel said.

Will murmured in my ear. "The blind leading the blind."

I giggled uncontrollably, and realized I'd already emptied my glass.

"Nikki, you're bubbling," Will said.

I laughed more, then tried to control myself by focusing on the horse as Orlando led him past.

The animal turned his head, and I noticed his far eye was ringed with white. I'd never liked this quality in a Thoroughbred. I'd known a few that could be a bit crazy.

"You see that wall eye?" I asked Will. "I don't think they should put Catalina on that horse, especially if she wears those spurs."

"You might be right," he said. "But he sure is a looker. Hey, Orlando, what's his name?"

"*Lo llaman*, Galaxy."

"Yes!" Catalina almost shouted. "He's got the star power. I am definitely riding this horse!"

"You might want to reconsider that," I said. "He might be too much for you." Everyone stared at me. Silence reigned until Catalina's mouth tightened in anger.

"Don't *ever* tell me what to do! You are nobody!"

She rushed at me, threw the contents of her flute in my face, then turned and snatched at Jamie's wrist.

"Take me to our hotel," she said, her tone imperious.

Stunned, Jamie stood still a moment.

"Now!" Catalina shrieked.

Her reaction seemed way over the top, as if serious self-esteem issues were at play.

Jamie shrugged. "As you wish."

His expression and tone were unreadable, but I didn't think he was happy. Who would be?

That evening Will and I walked to a cafe that Gabriel had recommended. It was crowded, so we took seats at the bar to order dinner.

The wall before us was mirrored, giving a nice view of the room behind. The glass also reflected the warm colors of the fine selection of liquor bottles shelved there.

"Don't look now," Will said, "but your buddy Catalina, just walked in. And look who she's with."

In the space between the blue and green of bottles of Bombay Sapphire and Tanqueray, I watched Catalina sit at a table with the mysterious light-haired man.

"Did you find out his name yet?" I asked.

"I couldn't find anything. I asked the home office techie, Brian, and he came up blank too. There's not one photo of anyone associated with this film that resembles our man over there."

The bartender leaned in, asked what we were drinking, and I said, "Wild Turkey 101, please."

"Make that two," Will said.

The man had us served in a jiffy, and I took a big sip of bourbon. I sighed with appreciation and hopped off my bar stool.

"Where are you going, Nikki?"

"To get his name."

"Will shook his head. "Hope your buddy doesn't throw another drink in your face."

"She doesn't have one yet," I said, and made a beeline for Catalina.

As I reached the table, I attempted a contrite expression. "Catalina, I'm sorry if I offended you earlier. You were right, you should ride Galaxy. He's the only horse we have whose beauty approaches yours."

Amazingly, I didn't gag over my words. Even more fantastic was her acceptance of them as her due. Her companion's smile never faltered and seemed genuine.

"You see what I'm telling you," she said to him, "I should ride Galaxy. This Stan person and even Gabriel, they don't know what they are doing. You will fix this, no?"

The man, who had light blue eyes, and very white skin, patted her hand. "Consider it settled, Catalina."

Something about his face was familiar. I stuck my hand out to him and said, "Hi, I'm Nikki Latrelle."

He smiled, rose from his chair and said, "Julio Vos. It is very nice to meet you." He sat and looked at his menu.

"Do you work on the film?" I asked him.

"No."

"Thank you for your apology, Nikki," Catalina said. "We should probably order our dinner now. So, until tomorrow?"

"Good night, Miss Latrelle," Julio said.

My dismissal was so clear that hanging around with more questions would be absurd, not to mention suspicious as hell.

I went back to Will and climbed onto my bar stool.

"His name's Julio Vos, and he says he doesn't work with the studio."

"Catalina didn't bite your head off?"

"No, but they were quick to get rid of me. And, Will," I said, "he was lying. He told Catalina he would fix it so she could ride Galaxy. How can he do that if he has nothing to do with the film?"

"Good question." He pulled his cell from a pocket. A moment later, he held the screen up to me. "Nothing comes up under his name, but look at this."

He had Googled the word Vos and he pointed to the second definition, which said the word was a Dutch surname for "Fox."

"If he's Dutch, that explains his coloring," I said.

"Wily like a fox, too," Will added. "I'll get together with Brian tomorrow and see what we can dig up on this guy."

Later than evening, as I stretched out on my hotel bed, I used my phone to look up the price of a Porsche Carrera. The convertible that Jamie was driving was called a Cabriolet. The base price was a hundred and twenty-six thousand.

"Damn," I said out loud. "I've never earned enough as a jockey to buy something like that."

And neither had Will. We were both competent riders but lacked the killer instinct and drive that the top five percent must be born with. My other problem was I cared too much about the horses to push as hard as some riders did.

I shut my phone off, plumped my pillows and lay back to sleep. "Maybe you should become a movie star," I said to the ceiling.

Then I couldn't stop giggling. Apparently, champagne and bourbon are a wicked combination.

# 11

The next morning, I had a killer headache. Two cups of coffee, several ibuprofens and one hot shower later, I struggled into my riding clothes and headed for Santa Anita.

When I arrived, Stan told me I was supposed to go to the base camp for wardrobe.

"How come I didn't hear about this yesterday?" I asked.

"I don't know. Just do it."

"Yes, sir." I did an about face and headed for the studio trailers, where a young woman with pink hair and a clipboard asked if I was Nikki Latrelle?

"That's me.

"Just call me Pinky," she said, and ushered me up three steps into a long white trailer.

Inside, much of the trailer's narrow space had double racks of clothes hanging on either side. A rolling ladder stood ready to access the top rows. A washer and dryer took up one end, along with an ironing board and a small setup for a seamstress. The room smelled like air freshener and laundry detergent.

The bright colors of jockey silks caught my eye. They reminded me of countless jockeys' rooms where I'd changed clothes at East Coast tracks. Every piece of clothing had a tag hanging on it, and when Pinky found my name on a set of silks, she handed them to me, along with a pair of white jockey pants.

"This stuff should fit you. What size shoe do you wear?"

I told her, and a moment later she handed me a pair of black leather jockey boots.

"Put this stuff on. There's a cubbyhole in the back for you to change, then head for the barn as fast as you can. When you're done, come back here, right?"

I nodded and rushed off to change. Moments later, amazed at how well everything fit me, I made tracks for the barn.

I did a double take when I saw Jamie. He looked more gorgeous than usual, and it took me a moment to realize the studio makeup artist had brightened the skin beneath his eyes, defined his eyelashes slightly and evened his skin tones. It was done so skillfully, that the makeup was almost invisible.

It occurred to me I wouldn't mind having the artist have a go at me. I could use a little brightening since my hangover was following me around like a dark cloud.

Greta and Jerry were already there, wearing bright silks and clean pants and boots. Several other exercise riders also stood in jockey apparel. Apparently, everyone but me got the memo.

Even Will was there in jeans and paddock boots, ready to ride out with us to keep an eye on things. Catalina flounced past him with the reddest lipstick I'd ever seen, which caused Greta and me to exchange an eyeroll.

Big surprise—the studio hadn't done their homework. Sure, female riders liked to look nice, but we were usually more concerned with staying alive and winning than wearing a boatload of cosmetics.

Gabriel gave me a wave, then disappeared into Stan's office, while I waited with Jerry and Greta for instructions.

The grooms were busy putting tack on several horses, including Galaxy. Stupid, since we'd had no time to feel the horse out.

A few minutes later, Gabriel reappeared and headed our way. "Okay, peeps. We're going to film a race. Jamie and Catalina have almost a minute of dialog before everyone loads into the gate. I need a realistic break, then a solid race around the track."

Listening to his words, I broke into a cold sweat. My reaction made no sense. I didn't do this before a real race, and this was just make-believe.

Gabriel, who'd paused to study papers on his clipboard, continued. "Okay, peeps," he said, waving at me and the other exercise riders, "you'll let Jamie and Catalina go to the lead at the top of the home stretch. Catalina will win. You got that?"

Everyone nodded.

I noticed that Jamie and Catalina also had papers on clipboards. They'd been studying them when I arrived. Maybe these were the famous "sides."

"Let's do this," Gabriel said.

An assistant took the clipboards from the two actors. The horses were led out, and Catalina got her wish. She was given a leg up onto the golden Galaxy. Jamie was put on Daisy Dan, and I rode Mystery Ride. Once mounted, we all rode to the track.

From her saddle, Greta leaned toward me and whispered, "I wish they'd put Jamie on Galaxy. That horse was whack-a-doodle in his stall earlier."

I shrugged. "What Catalina wants, Catalina gets."

"And she's wearing those *stupid* spurs," Greta said. "Can't someone tell these movie idiots that jockeys don't wear spurs?"

"Not unless you want a drink thrown in your face," I whispered back.

When we reached the track, we broke into a jog, then cantered the last eighth to the gate to warm up the horses.

Near the metal structure, Galaxy propped and stopped, throwing Catalina up on his neck. Bug-eyed, he snorted at a new addition near the gate. In fact, all the horses were taking a hard look at something that brought coal mining tunnels to mind.

Confused, I stared until I realized the studio had laid down parallel boards and fastened them with cross ties before putting down metal rails. A cart sat on the rails with a movie camera mounted on top.

Didn't our film director know *anything* about horses? "Gabriel, you'd better let these horses get used to this! If that cart's going to start rolling, you could have a stampede on your hands!"

Had he bothered to consult Stan about this?

Jamie booted his horse next to Galaxy and held the animal's reins, giving Catalina a chance to settle back into her saddle.

After a soothing pat on Galaxy's neck, Jamie said, "Nikki's right. Let the horses look at this thing. Then, roll the cart a little and let them get used to that. If you don't, this will become a total cock-up!"

Staring at the horses and frowning, Gabriel said, "I didn't realize they were so . . . *sensitive.*"

If Gabriel's look could kill, the horses would have dropped dead beneath us.

Ten minutes later, when the bugeyes and widened nostrils had dissipated, we got started. Jamie and Catalina rode alongside each other, led by members of the gate crew. The two actors spoke their lines as the camera and microphone rolled silently along next to them. They did this twice.

Then we were loaded into the gate. Handheld cameras filmed close ups of everyone, with most of the footage focused on Jamie and Catalina.

Racehorses don't like to stand too long in the gate. At least not with the expectation that at any moment the steel gates will crash open, the bell will ring, and jockeys will scream at them to run.

Galaxy and Mystery Ride grew more and more fractious, shifting anxiously and half rearing. The track crew was forced to open the gate behind Catalina and me and back us out. Our two horses took so long to settle, the ones waiting in the gate grew restless. The crew ended up backing everyone out, and we walked them in circles allowing them to stretch their muscles and relax.

Gabriel was not happy. Too bad.

We reloaded and waited for more film to be shot. Suddenly, the gate exploded open and we were off!

Mystery Ride went right to the lead with Galaxy hot on his heels. Jerry, urging his horse, ranged up alongside me a few strides later. The camera truck was off to our right.

With a quick glance back, I could see Jamie had a tight hold on Daisy Dan, keeping his horse behind the front runners this early in the race. The rest of the horses formed two packs behind us.

Old instincts are hard to fight. I was sitting on a ton of horse and wanted to win. But this was a movie, and my role was to let Catalina hit the wire first, with Jamie close behind.

By now, were into the far turn, with the top of the stretch almost upon us. I stood ever so slightly in my stirrups and took a better hold on Mystery Ride's mouth. It was like trying to stop a freight train. He wanted to go, and I wanted to let him.

Suddenly, Jamie had Daisy Dan's head even with Mystery Ride's withers. "Nikki, slow him down!"

I nodded. With one hand, I clamped the right rein to my horse's neck. With my left hand, I pulled as hard as I could. This forced his head to turn left, but in the film, the camera wouldn't see me doing it. Of course, I was aiming the horse for the rail, and if he didn't respond soon, I'd have to let go.

Instead of moving dangerously closer, Mystery Ride chose self-preservation and lessened his speed.

Two lanes to my right, Jerry was surreptitiously easing his horse to drop behind Catalina, who suddenly screamed at me.

"Let me by, damn it!"

Jamie, still alongside me, glanced back at Catalina. "Shake him up for God's sake. Move it, Catalina!"

The camera truck, still on our right side had moved farther away, to leave room for the two actors to come through. Thankfully, Mystery Ride was tiring, and since I wasn't urging him, he began to fall back.

In my peripheral vision, I saw Catalina's leg swing out, then slam back and rake Galaxy's side with a roweled spur.

Galaxy shot by me, his tail lashing angrily, his ears pinned straight back. Unbelievably, she raked him again. He shot to the right, slammed into the camera truck, bounced off and went down. Horrified, I realized Catalina had flown over his head. When Galaxy hit the ground, Catalina was beneath him, crushed by a thousand pounds of horseflesh.

# 12

Someone screamed, and riders shouted as they fought to stay clear of the wreck on the ground.

As I flashed past on Mystery Ride, Galaxy was struggling to his feet. Catalina was tangled in the horse's legs, and I thought I saw blood on the dirt. Then they were behind us.

The sight of them had spooked Mystery Ride, and he took off, almost ripping the reins from my hands. Frantically, I worked to slow him down, easing him to a jog and then a walk. When we turned back, Gabriel was climbing from the camera truck. His actions clumsy, his eyes dazed.

Catalina lay unmoving on the ground, and I was relieved to see the track ambulance had almost reached her.

Will had grabbed Galaxy's reins and was leading the horse close to me, where he sandwiched the nervous animal between our two horses. I patted Galaxy's neck and crooned soft nonsense as I noticed a gash on his shoulder. Glancing at the truck, the missing side view mirror told the tale.

By now, the EMTs had reached Catalina and were putting a brace on her neck, preparing to lift her onto a stretcher.

Gabriel stood unsteadily as he stared at her, his eyes filled with disbelief. Jamie dismounted and placed an arm around Gabriel's shoulder. He spoke quietly, apparently trying to comfort the distraught photographer. One of the extra riders led Jamie's horse away.

"Listen up, everyone," Will said. "There's nothing more we can do here. Let's get these horses in. Okay?"

Wordlessly, we turned and rode back toward the passthrough that would lead us to the backstretch barns.

The incident had left me disoriented. Once I reached the barn, I acted as if possessed, making sure the horses were cooled out, rubbed down, bandaged, and put away. I topped off water buckets, checked hay nets, even grabbed a pitchfork and helped Orlando and Ramon give the stalls a lick and a promise until the evening muck out.

Anything to stave off the images of Galaxy running into the truck, falling to the ground with Catalina crushed beneath him.

Except it didn't work. I kept seeing it happen again and again, just like the repeated image of Dave Wells' blood and brains splattering onto the camera truck's passenger window.

"Nikki, stop," Orlando said, taking the pitchfork from my hands.

Ramon stood next to him, a worried expression creasing his face.

"This our job. You upset. You should–"

"Nikki, take this." Greta had joined us, and she held out a can of beer. "You need it. God knows it helped me," she said, draining the rest of her Budweiser.

I blinked twice and took the can. I felt like a hole had opened inside me, sucking my energy through it, leaving me exhausted. Sinking onto a nearby hay bale, I leaned against the wall and sipped the cold beer.

"Bueno," Orlando said.

I nodded. "Thanks."

Glancing at Greta, I asked if there was any information about Catalina. "Do you know where they took her?"

"The ambulance guys said they were taking her to Methodist Hospital. I called the hospital but of course nobody would tell me anything."

"Have you seen Will?" I asked.

"He left. Said he had some phone calls to make."

As normal life slowly came back into focus, I remembered. Will was probably working on who this Vos guy was. Apparently, he hadn't let the events of the day rattle him. I looked around the shedrow. It appeared everyone else had gone.

Greta set her empty can on the ground and rubbed her eyes. "Seeing that happen to Catalina. It's really messed me up."

"Me too," I said.

"Do you think she's still alive?"

I shrugged. "Don't know, but like you said, we're not going to learn anything on the phone. How about we go to the hospital and see what we can find out?"

We drove fast and reached the hospital quickly. One elevator ride and an endless maze of tiled hallways later, we arrived at the intensive care nurse's station. A red headed nurse stared at me through her glasses when I enquired about Catalina.

"Are you a family member?"

"Yes," I lied. "I'm her sister, Nikki Espinosa."

"Your ID?"

"I drove her here," Greta said quickly. "She was so upset by the accident; she left her purse at home." Greta sounded calm and in command of herself, except one hand was twisting a blond braid like she'd rip it out.

"Please," I said, "Catalina's my sister!"

"All right." The nurse typed on her computer's keyboard. "She's still in surgery. If you wait, the doctor will speak to you when he can." Her face brightened. "Wait, there's Dr. Chen now." She pointed toward the end of the hall.

An Asian man wearing scrubs, stood with a guy who looked like . . . Julio Vos? But it was hard to tell from a distance.

"Thanks," I said to the nurse, and walked quickly toward the surgeon and the man I grew more certain was Vos. When he saw Greta and me coming, he turned and disappeared around a corner.

"Doctor Chen," I called, before he could evaporate around the same corner. "I'm Catalina's sister, is she . . ."

The man looked more exhausted than I felt. He sighed. "I was just talking to your uncle."

My uncle? Was Vos her uncle, or like me, had he lied to get information?

"Oh, right. Uncle Julio."

"How is she, Doctor Chen?" Greta asked.

"The surgery went well, but she sustained serious injuries. I'm concerned about internal bleeding. She's broken several ribs, ruptured her spleen. She may need additional surgery, but I believe in time, with physical therapy, she will recover."

"What about–"

"You sound like your uncle," he said, grimacing in disgust. "Only concerned about her ability to finish this film."

Realizing this was exactly what I'd been about to ask, I felt ashamed.

"Sorry," I said. "I guess this Hollywood stuff makes us seem pretty shallow." I straightened my shoulders. "Thank you for saving her life."

"You're welcome," he said tightly. He turned his back on us and vanished through a set of automatic doors.

"Well, I feel about one foot tall," I said.

Greta grimaced. "Me too."

"How about a late lunch and a drink?" I asked.

"I am so ready for a drink. Let's get out of here."

Greta and I sat at a table in the same café Gabriel had recommended to Will and me. She'd eaten most of her quiche, while I still picked at a salad niçoise. I knew I needed to eat, so, putting my fork down, I focused on the bread, butter, and bourbon. By the time I finished the glass of Wild Turkey, I was digging into the salad, surprised by my renewed appetite.

"We so needed to relax," Greta said. "It's been a hell of a day."

I nodded and looked at my watch. "I should probably check my phone."

I'd put it in airplane mode when we'd left the hospital, needing a break. Except for Greta, I hadn't wanted to talk to *anyone*. No sooner did I turn it on, then it chimed. I stared at the screen. Will.

"Hey," I said.

"Nikki, where are you? Everyone's looking for you."

"Who's looking for me?"

"Gabriel. Zalaya even called me trying to reach you."

"Why?"

"I don't know." His voice had an impatient edge.

"I'll call Gabriel now."

"You do that," he said, and hung up.

Apparently, the world didn't stop because I wanted it to. As if to confirm this thought, the waiter rushed to the table to collect our dishes.

"Care to see a dessert menu?"

"Don't need one", Greta said, "Bring me a slice of your chocolate cake."

He nodded, and I held up my empty bourbon glass. When he zipped off to get Greta's cake and my drink, I stared at the last roll and slathered it with but-

ter. Faster than I care to admit, I was swallowing the last bite and licking butter from my lips. Since I wasn't galloping horses every day, I might have to start
watching my weight.

But now, it was time to call Gabriel. When I reached him, his voice had a
dazed quality, like he was still trying to process the scene at the track. I felt bad
for him. It's one thing to know that horses can be dangerous, and another thing
entirely to see what a half-ton of horseflesh can do to the human body.

"Gabriel, it's Nikki. Will said you were trying to reach me?"

"Oh, Nikki, yeah. Have you got any acting experience?"

He was kidding right? Well one time I *had* feigned lust for a guy to distract
him from bidding on a horse he planned to slaughter. Shocking how good I'd
been at that. Then there was the day I'd faked being a gypsy and read people's
fortunes. I'd been good at that too. And I was a terrific liar. But I sure as hell
hadn't been to acting school.

A scary thought hit me. He couldn't want me to take Catalina's place. No,
of course not. I was being ridiculous.

"Nikki, *do* you have experience?"

"Not really. Why?"

"Zalaya is very disturbed about falling behind schedule. The man has been
desperate since Catalina was hurt. I think he wants you to take her place."

"That's crazy! I'm not an actress. He can get somebody else."

"Not an actress that can ride and is immediately available. He insists that I
get you to the sound stage as soon as possible. He's been calling you all afternoon!"

"What about one of the extras? Or one of the riders you've been using, like
Greta?"

"Greta is about as pretty as a blond bratwurst. Do you seriously see her playing opposite Jamie Jackson in a sex scene?"

"You don't need to insult people." My voice was tight with anger.

I looked at Greta, hoping she hadn't heard, but she was smiling at the waiter
who was placing her chocolate cake on the table. It was a big slice, and the scent
was rich and fragrant.

Wait, had Gabriel just said *sex scene*? No way was I letting anyone film me
like that with Jamie. Except, thinking about it, my body betrayed me. A warm

rush of desire slid through me, the hunger I'd been fighting since the first time I laid eyes on the guy. What was wrong with me?

"Listen, Nikki. We're all upset today. Greta's a nice girl, okay? But I hear you went to the sound stage the other night with Jamie. Zalaya was quite taken with you. You're pretty, there's a toughness about you that screams sex appeal, and when Zalaya saw the two of you together, he was entranced. I can see it myself. You're great on camera."

"You don't know that," I said.

"What do you think I've been doing since you got here, woman? I've been filming you."

"Oh."

"Where are you?" he asked.

"At the café across from my hotel."

"Leave *now*," he said. "Freshen up in your room. Put on some lipstick. Do your eyes. I'll pick you up in thirty minutes. *Tout de suite!*"

He disconnected before I could respond. I picked up my new glass of bourbon and drained it.

"They want you to replace Catalina, don't they?" Greta asked, her eyes sparkling with excitement.

"Yeah, but they're nuts. I can't do that."

"Aw, you'll be great," Greta said, waving a forkful of chocolate cake.

"But how does this work? Aren't we supposed to be members of the Screen Actor Guild? Surely if I take over Catalina's role, I'd have to be a member, right?"

Greta held up a finger, signaling me to wait while she finished a mouthful of cake. Then she spoke.

"The riders, including you, are all considered extras, but we don't need to be members. I read the rules and although every production must hire a certain amount of SAG extras for each day of filming, only the first thirty must be SAG extras. After that they hire non-union extras. That would be you, me, and Jerry."

"But," I said, "who are the thirty SAG extras?"

"Stan said they've had footage shot every day including race days. You know, make-believe fans in the grandstand and at the betting windows. That took care of the first thirty rule."

Greta's fork pushed into the cake again and ferried a large bite to her mouth.

My brain was working overtime, worrying about my new line of work. Suddenly I remembered lying in bed a couple of nights earlier and joking to myself about becoming a movie star. Apparently, the joke was on me.

Greta swallowed her cake and took a sip of water. "So, you'll need to talk to Zalaya about getting a SAG card, now that you're going to be a movie star."

I waved a dismissive palm. "This whole thing's ridiculous!"

"That may be, but aren't you supposed to be meeting Gabriel now?"

I grabbed my tote bag, tossed two twenties on the table, and double timed it to the hotel.

# 13

When I reached my hotel room, I washed my face, fluffed my hair with mousse, did my eyes, and applied lipstick. After pulling on a newer pair of skintight riding pants, I polished my paddock boots, changed tops and hot footed it to the lobby.

A bright red VW Beetle convertible idled outside the lobby doors, with Gabriel at the wheel. His long dark hair, swept back as usual, was covered with a black fedora. A band of dark red stitching enhanced the hat nicely, and a small red-and-white side bow finished the look. On anyone else, the fedora might have seemed effeminate, but on Gabriel, it was French, dashing, and totally masculine.

I climbed into the passenger seat, and we rolled out of the hotel's circular driveway.

"Cool hat," I said.

He smiled. "It's a Nick Fouquet."

Something else I'd have to look up.

Just another beautiful day in Arcadia, rolling along its sunny streets beneath palm trees, with the tangy lemon scent of eucalyptus wafting in and out of the car.

When we arrived at the sound stage, the guard waved us through the gate. Zalaya stood outside the studio door, his anxious expression breaking into a smile when he saw us.

I did not want the burden of being his savior. His expectations were upside down and hung on me like an albatross.

When he motioned us inside, I was shocked by the changes made since I'd last been there.

Towering above me was a peculiar looking two-story stud wall; peculiar because some sections projected out like boxes, and some projected inward like huge closets without doors. High above, steel cables supported the top edges of the walls. Electrical cords snaked across everything and slithered through holes drilled in the plywood.

I felt eyes on my back. Turning, I found Zalaya grinning at me, his eyes once again lit with enthusiasm.

"Come on!" he said, motioning me to follow him to the other side of the wall.

"She's going to love this," Gabriel said.

The back wall of the set was so large, it took a few moments to reach the other side. When I did, I was standing in Santa Anita's famous Chandelier room. Exact duplicates of the double staircases were at either end along with the mezzanine that ran across the top. The "huge closets" that had projected inward had turned into staircases—actual wooden structures I was sure I could climb.

The carpenters had put in a real parquet floor and blue couches like the ones I'd seen when I'd toured the grandstand with Will. The bar with a wall of mirrors behind it was there, too. And, of course, the chandeliers.

"This is incredible!" I said.

"My carpenters are like Santa's elves," Zalaya said proudly. "They can make anything."

"As long as there's money to pay for it," Gabriel whispered in my ear.

Until now, I hadn't wondered who or what was paying to produce this movie. I couldn't fathom how much this set cost. The place reeked with the smell of fresh paint, sawdust, glue, and new carpeting.

Further ahead, the elves were decorating another set, turning it into Santa Anita's exclusive event area called The Player's Club. They'd installed the polished wood floor, the leather couches, the betting counter and the huge monitors where gamblers watched multiple racetracks and sporting events.

"*Look* at this," I said. It's amazing!" I felt like a kid in a doll house.

My exhilaration seemed to have spread to Gabriel. He grabbed my arm.

"Come," he said. "You've got to see the *pièce de résistance!*"

He pulled me toward the far wall, currently hidden behind the Players Club. Clearing the club set, I saw yet another stud wall. It obscured a third of the building's back wall, the one that was all green screen. An open doorway in the stud wall had wood molding that was painted in the soft sea green so prevalent through the track grounds and stables.

When we stepped through it, we were suddenly standing on the grandstand's outside dining terrace. Before me was the track with the Santa Gabriel Mountains in the distance.

Still grinning, Zalaya spoke into a handset, and suddenly the track came alive, with a field of horses pounding around the far turn, racing down the stretch toward us. Clouds moved lazily in the sky, and a breeze rustled the fronds of the palm trees in the infield.

I pointed at the action. "Green screen, right?"

"See," Gabriel said, "I told you she was smart."

Zalaya nodded. "And pretty, too."

"And she's the real thing on horseback, like Jamie," Gabriel said.

Zalaya's enthusiasm suddenly evaporated into a frown. "I don't know why they insisted on using Ca . . ."

Gabriel took a verbal leap to cover Zalaya's unfinished sentence. "Jamie really likes you, Nikki. He's already said he loves the idea of you playing Fay."

"Fay?"

Zalaya, who'd been nervously rubbing the length of his soul patch, straightened shoulders and showed his teeth in a Hollywood smile. "Of course. You haven't read the script. Fay is the name of the jockey who plays opposite Jamie. You will be perfect as Fay!"

These two men were laying it on so thick, waders seemed an appropriate choice of apparel. The extraordinary experience of seeing Santa Anita materialize in a sound stage had almost made me forget why I was there. But their false flattery was bringing me back to earth real fast.

I waved a hand at the fake racetrack and the overhead grid of lights and cables. "I don't know anything about this world. I've never even acted in a school play."

"It doesn't matter," Zalaya said smoothly, "because you will be playing yourself. It's not like you must be *in character* and become someone else entirely."

"Exactly," Gabriel said. "Millie Mason has worked with dozens of new soap stars. She'll be a great coach for you."

By now Zalaya's smile was totally plastic. "Absolutely! She's excited that you're joining the team. She said the camera will *love* you."

"Look," I said, "I'll try it, but you better have someone else lined up for this role because I don't know if I can do it. And please, stop with the flattery. You don't make good hustlers."

Zalaya broke into a real smile. "Gabriel's right. You're no dummy, Nikki. But seriously, we're in a tight spot here. I'm grateful you're willing to try. So, let's do it."

Did he mean *now?*

He said something into his handset and the racing film went dark. I had no trouble hearing him say, "Get the Dillon set ready. We're doing an audition in two minutes. Yes, that's right. Is he here? Good."

My stomach clenched. I started to say, "Wait a minute," but before I got the words out, Zalaya and Gabriel were rushing me through the terrace door, across the cement floor, past the grandstand interior sets and the main entrance door. We entered an area I hadn't been in before and passed two bay doors you could drive a tractor trailer through. There were several heavy-duty lifters on wheels and a lot of scaffolding stacked nearby, and beyond that more stud walls, apparently the backs of additional sets.

"What's the Dillon set?" I asked.

"Dillon is Jamie's character in Final Furlong," Zalaya replied as we rounded the end of one of the stud walls and entered an apartment, or at least part of one. The furniture was modern, the decorating tasteful, with quiet earth tones. A big camera stood on a rolling platform with an operator behind it.

Jamie, wearing a white tee shirt and tight jeans, lounged on a leather couch. "You're late," he said.

He didn't look or sound like himself. He'd lost his British accent. He seemed rougher, meaner, almost threatening.

The look I threw Gabriel must have been desperate.

"Nikki," he said, "Jamie's in character. Dillon is not a nice guy. Just go with it, okay?"

I wasn't sure I wanted to.

"Fay's a lush," Dillon said with an ugly curl to his lip. "Get her a bourbon, and she'll do whatever you want."

I started to protest, but Zalaya burst out laughing. "This," he said to me, "is what it's all about. Dillon is here. Jamie's gone."

Zalaya put a gentle hand on my arm. "Go sit next to Dillon. We put together some lines. Read them, say them, we'll film it and see what we get."

The worlds of fantasy and reality were crashing together, leaving me disoriented and uncertain. I knew I didn't want to sit anywhere near this Dillon person, except, I reminded myself, it was Jamie.

With a sigh, I sat next to him and studied my script. But, I admonished myself, it's not called a script, it's called sides.

To my amazement a man rushed onto the set and handed me a tumbler of amber liquid and ice cubes. I could smell it almost before I had it in my hands. Bourbon.

I looked at Dillon. "Seriously?"

In an irritated, impatient voice, he said, "Drink it, bitch. You need it."

"Screw you," I said, and took a long sip. Warm as gold, it slid down my throat, sending a pleasant rush of heat to my stomach.

Or was the heat because Jamie had momentarily reappeared, the familiar smile on his lips. But his stare was intense and hungry. I wasn't sure who I was sitting next to.

Zalaya approached the cameraman, said something I couldn't hear, then came back and stood before Jamie and me. "Get up, you two. Stand about two feet apart and face each other."

I stood, still clutching my piece of sides, which indicated, we were having a fight.

Dillon let his flutter to the floor. Clearly, he didn't need it.

"That's fine, Nikki," Zalaya said, his tone kind and patient. "You hold onto your lines and we'll go through it as many times as you need before we run the camera. Okay?"

I nodded gratefully.

"Let's hear you, Nikki."

About as confident as a lost child, I said, "Look, you bastard, as much as I'd like to, I can't avoid you on race days. Outside of that, just stay the hell away from me."

I'd delivered the line with the emotion of a corpse. This wasn't going to work. I felt like an idiot.

Standing so close to Dillon didn't help either. Neither did his exaggerated eye roll.

"Again," Zalaya said.

By the fourth time Zalaya had me repeat the two sentences, I started to get pissed off, and it came through in my voice.

"Better! Once more and Dillon pick up your part this time."

The sides called for him to grab me roughly and kiss me, whereupon I was supposed to slap him and say, "Don't touch me."

Knowing this, I was as tense as a first-time jockey, locked in the starting gate, waiting for the bell to ring.

Staring at Dillon, I read my two sentences. I wasn't ready for how swiftly he whipped an arm around my neck, pulled me in, and forced a kiss that involved his tongue.

Stunned, I pushed him away, then remembered to say, "Don't touch me." The words were pathetically delivered.

Patiently, Zalaya said, "Again, and this time, Nikki, remember to slap him."

Dillon glanced at Gabriel, and the Frenchman joined the operator on the camera platform.

We did another take, that was marginally better, but still pitiful.

Dillon nodded at Gabriel and a red light blinked on at the camera. Before I could say my two sentences, Dillon moved into my space.

"This anger thing, is that all you've got?" He grabbed my arm with one hand, cupped my butt with the other and crushed himself against me, forcing my mouth open with a brutal kiss.

I reared back and slapped him so hard my palm stung. "Get off me, you bastard."

Dillon grinned.

"That's what I'm talking about!" Zalaya shouted. "Gabriel, you get that?"

"Oh yeah, I got it." Gabriel tipped his hat to me. "A star is born."

"Yeah, right," I said, disgusted with all of them.

"Come see," Gabriel said.

We went to the camera. A monitor attached to the camera lit up and played the scene. As pissed off as I was, a little thrill ran through me as I saw myself acting with Dillon.

Maybe I *could* do this.

# 14

By the time Gabriel dropped me at my hotel, I was so tired I was practically crawling through the lobby and onto the elevator. After calling room service, I soaked in a hot tub. When the food arrived, I was in bed, propped up with pillows and barely awake enough to eat. By nine p.m., my lights were out.

It was a restless night, filled with disturbing images. But the one that roused me at 5:30 a.m. was different. Whatever I'd been dreaming had been quite pleasant. No mangled bodies or blood. Instead, I woke up chasing broken fragments of a sexual fantasy.

Oh, great. I must have been dreaming about Jamie. But no, it was this Dillon character. Though he'd angered me, on a deeper level, he'd left me in a state of arousal. Damn him for clouding my judgement. Damn me for letting him.

Before I'd left the sound stage the previous evening, I'd asked Zalaya for a synopsis of the script. He'd said he couldn't give me that information. Instead, he'd given me my sides for this morning, which would be a repeat of what they'd filmed the day before.

Had it only been yesterday that Catalina had been injured?

I took a breath, stretched, and threw off the covers. Grabbing my sides off the night table, I read them, relieved to see Dillon's character had most of the dialog.

His words were a come-on. Totally obnoxious. My response consisted of sharp sarcastic comments. I was disappointed I wasn't supposed to hit him with my whip. But Zalaya was right, for this scene, at least, I would be playing myself.

I was sure I could handle the lines, but could I resist the force of Dillon's pull? The man was a heat seeking missile, and I didn't want to explode.

I didn't have to meet Pinky and the makeup artist until 8:30 and I needed some sanity time, something normal and safe. Grabbing my phone, I called Will.

"Are you awake?" I asked him.

"I am now."

"You ready for breakfast?"

"Do I have a choice?"

"No." I said. "I'm thinking hot coffee, pancakes and bacon.

Twenty minutes later I sat with Will in a small deli that served breakfast. It was a family-owned business, not a chain. The coffee was rich and smooth, the pancakes light and fluffy, the bacon crisp and delicious.

After I brought Will up to date with events since Catalina's injury, his lips grew tight and his eyes hardened. "So, you're going to do a sex scene with Jamie?"

I hadn't told him about the part where Jamie had been so rough. But Will could always read me like a billboard. Something in my voice or eyes always gave me away.

"Look," I said. "As far as I'm concerned, I don't want to be in a scene anymore graphic than when Rhett Butler carried Scarlett O'Hara up the stairs and the screen went dark." I was such a liar.

"Come off it, Nikki. Any idiot can see you have the hots for the guy. Listen, it's none of my business anymore, is it?"

I was ashamed of the lost feeling that washed through me. Did I still want Will to love me? Was I that greedy and selfish? I was the one who'd broken it off.

Unable to answer him, I took a sip of coffee, then pushed a piece of pancake around my plate. The room was filling with more people and the clatter of plates and silverware grew with the sound of conversation.

"So," he said, "about Vos."

I grabbed his words like a lifeline. "What did you find out? Could he be Catalina's uncle?"

"I don't know. Brian and I didn't know to look for that connection. We'll find out, but right now, what I *can* tell you is this. Vos is a prominent Panamanian businessman. He owns a company that produces specialty luggage and luxury goods that sell at international airports. He has no known record or ties to crime. Apparently, he's simply a successful businessman."

I ate several bites of pancake and began munching on a piece of bacon.

"What was interesting," he said, "is we discovered Vos is one of the producers of Final Furlong."

"You mean he's provided funding for the movie?" I asked.

"Yeah. That explains why we've seen him hanging around and why Jamie saw him in the Estrella studio in LA."

"That means Vos is one of the people that Zalaya answers to," I said. "Maybe one of the reasons he's so concerned about falling behind schedule. If he loses funding, he loses the movie."

"No flies on you, Latrelle."

"But I thought Vos was Dutch. His skin is so fair. Aren't Panamanians darker?

"Listen," he said, "Brian filled me in on Panama. When they built the canal, large numbers of people, mostly Chinese, emigrated to Panama for the work. He said thousands of Afro-Caribbean workers were also recruited from Jamaica, Barbados and Trinidad. And there were Dutch and German contingents, too."

"It's always the same," I said, "everyone follows the money. But I bet Catalina *is* Panamanian. She could be part Dutch and part Hispanic. It would explain those exotic looks. She never said she was from Mexico, only that she rode races there."

Which as far as I was concerned was a big fat lie.

Will's expression grew thoughtful, "You know, I bet Vos is her uncle. It explains how she got the job, which was something I couldn't figure out."

"Me either," I said.

"And now you've got the job, which is good. Puts you in a position to know more about what's going on inside Estrella."

I wiped a bit of bacon grease from my lips. "The thing I'd like to know is what was up with Vos's two companions that night. The ones in the restaurant and outside the sound stage. They were hard looking men and they spooked the hell out of Zalaya."

"Vos runs a big company, Nik. They could just be business associates."

"I don't buy that. You didn't see how worried Zalaya was."

"Then keep an eye out and, for God's sake, remember to watch your back."

He sounded so serious, I wondered if he knew something he wasn't telling me.

"I got to go. I'm meeting somebody," he said.

When I asked who, he said, "I'll see you later, Nik." He put some money on the table and left.

I picked up my sides and tried to memorize the lines.

At 8:30 Pinky handed me my boots and a set of silks like the ones Catalina had worn. I'm not overly superstitious, but I felt weird about putting them on.

"Aren't these the same ones that—"

"Lord, no." Pinky said. "Catalina's silks were destroyed; besides they would have been too big on you. We made up new sets."

I nodded, feeling relieved.

"Take these and go to the silver trailer." Leaning out her door, she pointed to a long shiny trailer. "Sally will do your makeup, okay?"

I marched to the silver trailer and knocked on its door. A thin, dark haired woman with no makeup ushered me inside. She had me change into the silks, put a plastic drape over them, and sat me in a chair.

Out of nowhere, a flash of grief hit me. The only other person who'd done my makeup was my friend Carla. She'd taught me a lot about life, then I'd watched her be murdered. It was a horrible memory that blindsided me at unexpected moments. Compartmentalizing the bad stuff didn't always work for me.

"Look," I said, "don't put too much make up on me, especially that bright red lipstick. I've been a jockey, and that much stuff on my face is totally unrealistic.

"As you wish."

She did her work, using a soft red lipstick, and subdued eye makeup. When I looked at my reflection, I had to admit I looked really good, not fake.

"You have a pretty face," she said. "And you are much more athletic looking than Catalina. You fit the part well."

Before I could reply, a car horn sounded outside.

"That will be your ride," she said. "Good luck."

I thanked her, left the trailer, and climbed into the waiting Lincoln Town Car.

"This is ridiculous," I told the driver when he drove me the short distance to our stable gate. "I could have walked."

"If it's in your contract, then you gotta be driven, okay? Union rules."

I started to say I wasn't a union member, thought better of it, and swallowed the comment.

Once I walked beneath the queen palm, I could see Orlando and Ramon getting the horses ready. Colorful as peacocks, the extra riders stood in a group.

Jerry, in purple and bronze silks, was grinning at me. "Oh, look. It's our new star!"

"Don't give me a hard time, Jerry," I said. "I'm nervous enough as it is."

"Ah, you'll be great," Greta said.

I noticed the other riders were looking at me differently. Suddenly, I was no longer part of the gang, and I didn't like it.

I saw everyone turn and look behind me. Dillon was walking toward us. No question it was Dillon. His face was hard, his eyes cold until they swept over me. He moved right into my space, so close only I could hear him.

"I like the red on your lips. I'll get to them later." He turned and walked across to where Gabriel was standing.

The two of them laughed which left me burning with unspoken sarcastic comments. Dillon had played me to set his scene. Maybe he simply wanted the movie to be a success, but I didn't like the way he'd left me feeling.

Gabriel waved me into Stan's office. As usual, a bottle of Crown Royal stood on Stan's desk next to a glass that was still wet inside. He rose from his chair, mumbled good morning, and limped out.

Gabriel opened a folder on the desktop and had me sign a bunch of papers from the Screen Actors Guild. The parts for my personal information and ID were already filled out.

"Shouldn't I read this?" I asked.

"I'm afraid there isn't time, Nikki. Besides, I've read it. It's all standard boiler plate. Just sign the papers."

I did, and when we walked onto the shedrow, the grooms had already tacked up the horses. Moments later, I was on the flighty Gazelle. This was fine, because compared to Jamie's "Dillon" character, handling her was a cake walk.

When our group reached the track, the rolling camera cart had been set up again. The camera truck was there, with the new assistant at the wheel. Gabriel was fiddling with the camera cart.

I pulled my crumpled sides from my pocket and read my lines one last time. Moments later, I was riding next to Dillon, the camera cart rolling beside us.

When Dillon spoke his first lines, they sounded just as obnoxious as they had looked on paper. I shot my lines right back. Then we were in the gate. Dillon was so real to me; I had no problem showing my dislike through my tone of voice and body language.

I expected Gabriel to ask for another take. Instead, the bell rang. We erupted from the gate. I steadied Gazelle and let Jerry and another guy take the lead. The camera truck rolled beside us with Gabriel riding shotgun and working the controls on the truck's dash.

At the top of the stretch, I shook Gazelle up a bit. She gained ground, passed Jerry. The other rider and Dillon were ahead of me. Dillon looked back.

"I thought you knew how to ride," he yelled.

I took a cross with my reins, Gazelle changed leads, and I set her down. We flew past the other two just before the wire. Gabriel got his exciting finish, and Dillon got my middle finger.

# 15

Back at the barn, the Estrella caterers were serving lobster salad, fresh fruit, and warm baguettes. The riders and grooms were digging in like they hadn't eaten for weeks. Then again, when was the last time any of us had the money for lobster?

Gabriel was so pleased with his successful one-take shoot, he opened another bottle of champagne. Grinning, he handed me a flute of golden bubbles.

"Nikki, you're a natural!" His voice was too loud, as if he was making an announcement.

"Stop with the flattery," I whispered.

"No, I'm serious. I watched the film. Zalaya saw it too. Your displeasure with Dillon is marvelous, *convincing*."

"That's because he totally pissed me off," I said.

Dillon raised a glass to me. "Glad to be of service, anytime. You are one hot babe when you're mad."

The look that accompanied his words was so wolfish, I took a step back. He ran his tongue over his lower lip.

"For God's sake, Jamie," I snapped, can you stop with the Dillon act?"

"Can't do that, babe. Besides, I think you like it."

"I sure would," Greta whispered over my shoulder. Stepping forward, she glanced at me, her eyes lit with mischief. "Nikki, you're blushing." She drained her flute and headed back to the buffet table for more lobster.

Some of the riders were staring at me. What, because I was going to star in a stupid film? Get a life, people.

Will was watching from the shedrow, shaking his head, leaving me with a strong desire to exit stage left. I could almost hear him thinking, "Bobby Duvayne all over again. She just won't learn."

*Get a grip,* I told myself. You're supposed to be happy about all this, not paranoid.

The caterers began clearing the buffet table. I grabbed a bottle of water before they could remove it, glad the others had finished off the champagne. I needed to keep a clear head because Zalaya and Gabriel had plans for me that afternoon.

I exited past the Australian willow, ignored my driver lurking inside the Lincoln, and walked to my trailer. During lunch, Gabriel had given me the keys to what had been Catalina's trailer, and I wanted to check it out.

I unlocked the door and stepped inside. Elegant, thick cream carpeting covered the floor. Taupe leather couches and chairs formed a grouping, and a divan for napping lay against one wall. A long white counter with a lighted mirror offered a cornucopia of makeup and hair products. Beyond it was a bath. Its shelves were loaded with fluffy white towels, and a plush robe hung on the wall.

Wasting no time, I luxuriated in a hot shower, amazed to find Hermes perfumed soap and shampoo. I could get used to this.

Leaving the bath, I discovered that someone had been in the trailer and laid out the clothes I was to wear that afternoon. How many people had keys to this place, anyway?

Outside of the bath's bolt lock, privacy was not an option. At least not one I'd count on. My phone dinged with a text. I was expected in makeup in fifteen minutes.

In case housekeeping, hair, makeup, my driver, or worst of all, Jamie in full "Dillon" mode, entered in my trailer, I locked the bathroom door and changed in there.

The silky blue dress they'd given me matched my eyes and fit perfectly. How do they do that? Except it was cut a bit low for comfort and the pushup bra they'd left worked too well. I caught myself blushing in the mirror.

Stepping into strappy heels, I clacked down the trailer's steps and headed for makeup. Welcome to Hollywood.

Perched like a nervous bird on the edge of a couch, I listened to Millie Mason's beautifully modulated voice as she gave me a brief lecture on acting. We were sitting on the set for the Player's Club, drinking sparkling water. A tray of lemon wedges and oatmeal cookies sat on the coffee table before us.

It was totally amazing to me that I was being coached by this tremendously popular soap star.

"Remember," she said, "acting is not about speaking your lines, it's about feeling the emotions your character is feeling. Nikki, once you know your lines, you need to make choices. What does your character want, what do they not want? Why?"

She paused to squeeze a wedge of lemon into her water before continuing. "When you're in character, you decide what you're afraid of, what you want the audience to know and what you don't want them to know. Make sense?"

"It does," I said. "But it's got to take a long time to develop that kind of skill."

"Not necessarily," she said. "Zalaya thinks you're a natural."

"That's only because Dillon truly annoyed me," I said.

"Are you sure?"

The strong odor of glue, sawdust, and new carpeting had diminished. Between my Hermes, whatever delicate scent Millie was wearing, and the tang of fresh lemon, our little sphere on the couch was quite pleasant.

I thought about her question. "I think being angry was the reason I delivered what they wanted."

"The character of Dillon," she said, "is a tough man, who is gorgeous, irresistible, but also a sexual predator. That can present conflict that's hard for any woman to deal with. I'd bet those emotions played a big part, right?"

She tilted her head to one side, waiting for my response.

"The truth is," I said, "I'd like to smack him. But I wouldn't throw him out of bed, either."

Millie emitted a peal of laughter. "I know exactly what you mean," she said. "I'm sure you'll do at least as well as Catalina."

"But I don't know *anything* about acting," I said.

"My point exactly, dear." The amusement in her eyes was telling.

I felt bad for Catalina, who I'd heard was out of a second surgery and doing okay. I didn't like that I'd received this chance due to her injury. But it wasn't like I could undo what had happened.

Millie and I sat for another twenty minutes or so, while she explained that in *The Final Furlong,* she was the owner of a top horse, Reddinger was her trainer, and, of course, Dillon and I were the jockeys who sparred with each other, doing whatever it took to get the ride on her champion horse.

Grabbing a cookie, I said, "Thanks for telling me. Everyone is so close-mouthed about the script; I've been totally in the dark."

"Really," she said, "it's ridiculous how paranoid the studios are about hiding their story lines. God forbid there's a leak."

I nodded and munched on my cookie. Just when I was feeling relaxed, she said, "Here comes your predator."

He wore a sleeveless, black leather vest and leather pants they must have stitched him into. He had one silver earring and a braided silver necklace. Every item was expensive, tasteful, and designed to set off his long legs and muscular arms. Not to mention his blond hair and blue eyes.

*I could get into a lot of trouble with this man.*

I was relieved to see Dexter Reddinger walk onto the set behind Dillon. It gave me something else to look at.

Coming from a modern western TV show, he fit the role of racehorse trainer perfectly, like a Wayne Lucas or Bob Baffert, top trainers who'd started out with quarter horses. Wardrobe had given Reddinger a southwestern flair with jeans, cowboy boots, and a suede jacket.

Millie bloomed pink as Reddinger sat beside her on the couch. With his longish silver hair, beard, moustache, and those piercing blue eyes, I could understand her reaction. In this fantasy world, no wonder actors and actresses hooked up.

Then Zalaya walked in, and the energy in the room diminished. His hair seemed greasier than usual, and he looked like he was worried and trying to hide it.

His hands held a thin stack of sides, and he passed them out to the four of us. Once free of the papers, he rubbed his long soul patch with twitchy fingers.

Quickly, I read my lines, then glanced at the ones on Millie's page. Looked like we were doing a confrontational scene.

Suddenly, bright lights burned overhead, and I realized there were crew members on the scaffolding near the ceiling. Some of them held what I thought of as boom mikes, but really, I had no idea what they were called.

Gabriel strode in, and the assistant cameraman rolled in behind him on the big camera platform. Extras appeared and took their places on other chairs and at the betting counter where people acting as betting ticket sellers stood ready to go into action.

It must have taken about ten minutes, but for me, it happened so fast, I barely had time to get nervous.

At first, I stumbled on my lines, but Millie was patient, Reddinger charming, and Dillon so obnoxious, I turned the anger he generated into the power I needed to focus and do it right.

We stopped filming around six that evening. Gabriel and Zalaya seemed pleased. Millie told me that for a beginner with no acting experience, I'd done a great job, Reddinger said I fit the part well, and Dillon said nothing.

The set dimmed, the extras left, and so did, Millie, Reddinger, and Dillon. Zalaya and Gabriel were still standing behind the big camera, watching a replay on the camera's small monitor.

Instead of leaving, I had sagged onto the couch to catch a mental breath, soak up the feel of the set and replay my own mental tapes of the last few hours.

"Nikki," Gabriel called, "I just sent today's film to the viewing room. Come watch it on the big screen with me."

I said I would and followed him out of the Player's Club, through the Chandelier Room set, toward the bay doors, lifters and scaffolding. A door I hadn't noticed before was set in the wall opposite the bay doors. Through it, a hallway I hadn't known existed was to the left. It ran along the entire wall.

Glancing down its length, it appeared to go as far as the green wall. Probably a way to get around the building without disturbing a live shoot.

Gabriel turned right, passing by two offices, before entering a small theatre. I was amused to see La-Z-Boys chairs with cup holders and those flip-up leg rests. The chairs faced a screen on one wall. A control panel was set up behind them.

A pile of boxes, duffel bags, and carryalls were heaped in one corner.

"Sorry about the junk," Gabriel said. "I've been trying to go through that mess for days."

While Gabriel fiddled with the control panel, I wandered around the room, passing by the junk pile. Glancing down, two words stopped me cold. I leaned over a carryall to make sure. Its ID tag read, "David Wells." The mental image of his murder, the gunshot to his head. It was so real, for a moment, I couldn't move or speak.

"Gabriel," I managed to say, "there's something here that belonged to David Wells. Have the police seen this?"

"*Mon Dieu,* I didn't know that was there! Those things were transferred from the Hollywood office a few days ago."

I knew I shouldn't, but I pulled the zipper open and studied the contents. Gabriel rushed to look over my shoulder. A camera and a small case containing flash drives were inside.

"I wondered what had happened to those," Gabriel said. "There's one missing with Millie and Reddinger. I should check these before we watch today's work."

"Of course," I said.

He grabbed the three or four flash drives and inserted one into a slot in the control panel. A video of Zalaya started playing. He was talking to a Hispanic man in what looked like an alley. When the Hispanic man turned his head, I saw he was missing an ear.

Gabriel's breath drew in sharply. "*Mon Dieu,*" he whispered. With trembling hands, he shut down the video.

"What?" I asked. "Who is that?"

The blood had drained from his face. His words came out strangled. "Forget you saw this! *We* did not see this. No wonder they killed him."

"But who is that? Why did they kill Wells?"

"I will not talk about this," he said. "I want you to leave."

When I started to speak, he yelled, "Leave now, Nikki. Get out! "

Speechless, I watched him remove the flash drive. He handled it like it was a scorpion stinging his fingers.

When he realized I hadn't moved, the look he gave me was so full of terror, I ran from the sound stage, hurried to my waiting Lincoln, and told the driver to make tracks.

# 16

On the way out, my driver stopped and waited for the security gate to open. I looked back at the cinder block sound stage, wondering what the hell was Gabriel so afraid of. Who was this man with the missing ear?

As I was about to turn away, movement at the corner of the building caught my eye. A dark-haired man with a gold necklace was walking toward the parking lot. I scanned the parked vehicles and wasn't surprised to see a dark SUV with heavily tinted windows. With another look back, I saw a second man with a diamond glittering on his hand. He caught up with the first guy.

Had to be the same two thugs. Where had they been? I pictured the long, hidden hallway on the far side of the building. Had they been in there? Perhaps there was an exit from that corridor out the back of the building.

The man with the flashy ring was waving his hands in agitation as he spoke to the gold necklace man. They broke into a run, heading for their SUV.

My driver retrieved my phone from the guard, and when the security gate finally opened, I leaned forward. "I have a screaming headache. My -- my medication is back at my hotel. Would you mind stepping on it, please?"

I expected him to say he wouldn't break the law on account of a headache, but the limo leapt forward with enough power to momentarily pin me to the back seat.

Behind us, the SUV was waiting its turn for the security gate to open. Hopefully, since my limo also had dark tinted windows, they had no idea I was in it. Besides, what would anyone want with me?

I sent Will a text saying I was on my way back and urgently needed to talk to him at the hotel. I wanted to talk to him in person, not leave a text that someone might read.

My phone dinged with a return message. He was in a meeting but would be at the hotel in forty-five minutes.

Wardrobe expected me back to leave the clothes I'd worn to the sound stage. But what the heck, I'd drop them off in the morning when I went to get my silks. Santa Anita had one more dark day where we could film on the track, and then, we'd most likely work at the sound stage during the three days of live racing.

The Lincoln turned in the wrong direction. I stared at the driver's face in his rear-view mirror.

"What's going on?" I asked. "You should have made a left."

"Sorry, I forgot to tell you. You've been moved to a suite at the Marriott."

"But my stuff! I need to get my things."

"It's taken care of, Ms. Latrelle. Pinky collected your personal items, packed them and moved them for you."

"It would have been nice," I said, "if somebody had told me."

"You'd have to take that up with Frank Zalaya."

Sure, I'd get right on that.

A few minutes later, we arrived at the Marriott. As I started to climb from the car, the driver hopped out, came around, and handed me a plastic cardkey tucked into a little envelope.

"Your room number is written on the outside here," he said, pointing at the scribbled digits.

I thanked him, grabbed my tote, and hurried inside. A quick glance around the parking lot showed no sign of the dark SUV. But they hardly could have gotten there ahead of us, could they? We'd zipped along too fast for them to have arrived first. Besides they didn't know I was in a different hotel. Once I was inside the lobby, I still stared through the glass doors to make sure the SUV didn't appear.

Gabriel's fear had found a way to burrow under my skin and I didn't like it. I was being paranoid, overreacting.

Inside the elevator, I pushed my floor number and waited impatiently. When the door opened, I scurried down the carpeted hall, found my room, and once inside, I shut, bolted and chained the door.

The cleaning staff had been busy. The room was spotless, and the scent of their spray air freshener lingered. Almost like a man's cologne.

With a sigh of relief, I sat on the arm of a large couch for a moment and sur-veyed the room. Aside from the couch, there were two overstuffed armchairs, a cabinet bar, and a wide screen television. A half bath was close to the entry door. In the opposite direction, I saw a foyer that led to the bedroom and main bath. Good thing I wasn't paying for this set up.

Rising from the couch, I pushed through the partially open bedroom door and headed for the closet to see if my things were inside. Behind me, the bed-room door clicked shut.

My breath sucked in as I whirled. A man stood behind me. He must have been hiding behind the bedroom door. My heart pounded as I saw his face. An ugly smile revealed a gold tooth that glowed in the overhead light. The smile didn't travel to his eyes. They were cold, dark, and without emotion.

A long, jagged scar ran up the side of his neck, a red arrow pointing to the deformed opening that had once been an ear. His hand appeared relaxed and loose as it held a long, serrated knife.

My fingers grew so cold with fear, they felt numb. "What do you want?" I hardly recognized my voice. How could he know I would be in this room? Was someone at Estrella working with this guy?

He put a finger to his lips.

"Who are you?" I asked.

His mouth compressed into a tight line. He grabbed my wrist. I was no match for the strength in his thick muscular body. He tossed me on the bed. His knee pressed into my chest, pinning me down. He held the knife against my throat, and once again put a finger to his lips.

When I clamped my mouth shut and gave him a tiny nod, he withdrew the knife from my throat and backed off. His cologne made me want to gag. Stupid to have mistaken it for air freshener when I'd entered the room. I could have bolted, I could have–

Someone knocked on the door. God don't let it be Will. This monster would kill him. But it couldn't be Will. He thought I was at my old hotel.

The man grabbed my wrist again and whipped me off the bed like a ragdoll. Towing me to the entrance door, he stared through the peep hole. With a grunt, he undid the locks and opened the door.

Gold Necklace and Diamond Ring entered the room. Their suit jackets were unbuttoned, revealing their holstered handguns. Who had told these men where I was? My driver? Zalaya?

My one-eared tormentor slid his knife into a sheath on his hip. He buttoned his coat, hiding the knife. He removed a folded cap from his pocket. When he shoved it on, it hid the gruesome hole in his head.

I was behind him and couldn't see his expression. But some soundless message passed from him to the other two men, because they nodded.

Gold Necklace said, "We'll take care of it."

Without a sound, or a last glance at me, the one-eared man left the room. Diamond Ring locked and bolted us in, then turned to me.

I was so afraid I thought my knees would buckle. To control my rising panic, I forced myself to do a mental inventory of the two men.

Both were swarthy, with black hair and brownish-black eyes. Gold Necklace was the uglier of the two. He had severe acne scars on his face and a nose that had been broken too many times. Diamond Ring might have been attractive if there'd been a trace of charity or kindness in his eyes. I pegged him as the smarter and nastier of the two.

He nodded toward the couch. "Sit."

I did, and he sat next to me. Gold Necklace leaned against the wall near the entry door. His eyes never left me.

Diamond Ring removed his handgun from its holster and pointed it at my face. "We had a little talk with your buddy Gabriel. He begged us to convince you to keep your mouth shut. He knows what will happen if you don't."

"I, I don't even know what I'm not supposed to talk about."

"Don't play games. You saw this." His other hand withdrew a flash drive from his pocket."

I dropped the lie. He'd obviously been close enough to overhear us when Gabriel had played the video.

"Why would I say anything? I don't know who that is that just left. I've never even heard him speak." And I hoped I never would.

The man seemed to study his large diamond before meeting my gaze. "My friend who just left is very unhappy he was forced to come here. He does not like to be seen."

Probably, a smart comment like, "So why did he come?" wouldn't go over well.

Both men watched my face as if it might give something away. But I didn't know anything. If I tried to convince them of this, I'd only dig myself in deeper. So, I said nothing.

Diamond Ring guy leaned closer to me, stroking the side of my face with the steel barrel of his gun. "We know a lot about you, Ms. Latrelle."

I remained silent.

"For instance, we know that Mr. Marshall is a lover and a friend. A confidant, no? We know he works for the TRPB, and we know that organization has ties to the FBI." He smiled at me. "Still, you are an artist, and we want you to have your role in this movie. It would be a shame to waste such an attractive, young talent."

His smile was a dead thing. He would never make an actor. He didn't give a flying fuck about me or my career. Why did he care about the movie?

My phone rang. I didn't move and the call went to voice mail.

Diamond Ring slipped the flash drive back into his jacket, withdrew a folded photo from his breast pocket, and handed it to me. "You wouldn't want your friend, Marshall, to end up like this would you?"

I unfolded the photo and stared. Nausea rose in my throat. David Wells lay on a slab in what must be the Arcadia morgue. These people were connected if they'd been able to obtain a crime photo from the morgue. Remembering Gabriel's terror when he'd seen the one-eared man in the video, I shrank against the back of the couch. A whimper escaped me.

"Don't be frightened, Ms. Latrelle. Just keep your mouth shut. Not one word to Mr. Marshall or anyone else. Not even Gabriel Dubois. Do you understand?"

I nodded.

He pushed the gun's barrel to my throat. "Let me hear you say it."

I had to swallow before the words would come out. "I won't say anything."

"Good," he said, "we have an understanding. You are to act normally and finish *The Final Furlong*. Yes?

"Yes," I whispered.

"Hand me your phone."

When I did, he nodded at Gold Necklace guy, who left his post by the wall and handed me an iPhone identical to my own. He took my old one and it disappeared into his jacket.

"We took the liberty of borrowing your phone earlier."

For a moment I was confused. But of course, they could have taken it after I relinquished it to the guard at the sound stage. Was everyone in on this? I wish I knew what "this" was.

"Your new phone," he said, "has the same number and information as that stored on your old one." He touched my cheek again with his gun. "But we will know who you call, what you say, and where you are. If you try to disable the phone, we will know. That would be quite unpleasant for you and Mr. Marshall. Do you understand?"

"Yes," I said. The word came out like the mewl of a kitten.

He stood, put his gun away, and the two men left me alone in my suite. The scent of the one-eared man's aftershave still lingered in the air.

I clapped my hand over my mouth, ran to the bathroom and vomited. When I was finished, I was too weak to rinse out my mouth. I sank to the floor, shivering.

# 17

Most people, at one time or another, have collapsed on a bathroom floor after they've been violently nauseous. Food poisoning or stomach flu will lay a person out.

But I'd been sick with fear and had no time to coddle myself. Some of the chill had left me and my hands had almost stopped shaking. I climbed to my feet, clutching the sink.

Scanning the bath, I saw that when Pinky had moved my stuff to the Marriott, she'd left my toiletries on the sink counter. First thing I grabbed was my toothbrush and toothpaste. After that, and a face wash, I felt close to human.

My new phone had rung a few times when I'd been too sick to move. When I emerged from the bathroom, I grabbed it from where I'd left it on the couch. Four messages from Will.

Where was I? Was I all right?

Preparing myself to lie, I took a deep breath, and called him.

"Hey," I said.

"Nikki, what happened to you. They said you're no longer registered at our motel. Where are you?"

I explained about the hotel upgrade and apologized for not reaching him sooner.

"That's fine, but you said you had something urgent to tell me. So, tell me."

I wasn't about to say I couldn't talk because my phone was bugged, and some really bad people were probably listening to us. That would put him right over the edge.

So, instead, I said, "That was a mix up. There's no problem. I was just confused about something. Really, it's nothing." *Shut up, Nikki, you're babbling.*

And Will knew me too well, knew I tended to babble when I was trying to hide something.

"Whatever you say." His voice was harsh and followed by silence. I started to say something, but he cut me off. "You know what? I need to talk to you anyway. I'm coming over there."

"No, Will. I had a tough day of filming. I really need to take a nap. Maybe I'll see you later." But he'd already hung up.

Searching the room for telltale signs of my earlier trauma, I saw the morgue photo of Dave lying on the couch. I grabbed it and shoved it under a cushion before rushing into the bathroom.

In the mirror, my face was drained of color. Damn, I'd washed off all the stage makeup. Grabbing my kit, I put on some blush and a bit of lipstick. Better, but I still looked like I'd been dragged through the house of horrors. I made myself smile. It was almost as scary as the dead thing I'd seen plastered on Diamond Ring's mouth.

Stepping from the bathroom I spotted a radio on the counter and turned it on. Someone had left it on an oldies station, and it was playing one of my Mom's favorite songs by the Stones, "Gimme Shelter." *Perfect.* My feet started moving, and I danced like a fool to the song, shouting along with Mary Clayton, "Murder, it's just a shot away," letting the fear slide from me into the song.

By the time I heard a knock on my door, I was singing at the top of my lungs, "It's just a kiss away, kiss away, kiss away!"

I turned the radio off and stared through the peep hole. Will stood outside. When he came in, he gave me his *what is with you* look.

"Were you singing about Jamie Jackson?" he asked.

"No. I just felt like singing. Is that a crime?"

"Nope. But if you know something you're not telling me, *that* would be a crime in my book."

"I don't know anything," I said. "I told you, I was just confused about something."

"About what?"

I couldn't think of a good lie and just stared at him.

"Damn it, Nikki. I got you this job to be an informant. Then I told you being on the inside with the Estrella production could produce information. Apparently, it has, and for some reason you're withholding it. Are they paying you money to be quiet?"

"No one's paying me money to be quiet!"

"That may be, but you're on their payroll now, and I'm sure it's way more than the TRPB can afford."

Will has always had a soft quiet voice. It was one of the things I loved about him. He so rarely raised it in anger. But he did now.

"You're lying to me Nikki. I *know* you. A man was murdered! You mentioned some slimy characters you'd seen, but there hasn't been another word from you about any of it."

I recoiled from his anger, taking a step back and sinking onto the couch. The scent of the one-eared man still lingered. Of their own accord, my arms wrapped protectively around my middle.

"I can't."

Will shook his head, curling his lip in disgust. "Bullshit! Can't means won't. We don't need you working for us if you're going to lie."

He paused, rubbing his temple as if attempting to calm himself.

"Look, Nikki, I know your childhood. I know how important it is to you to never go back to the poverty you suffered after your mother died. I've been *trying* to do you a favor."

His anger blossomed again, reddening his face. It made me cringe.

"Do me a favor, Nikki, go ahead and 'kiss away' with your movie man. Maybe he'll make you a star too. Just be careful you don't wind up a *shooting* star. So, good luck with it!"

He turned away from me and strode to the door. It slammed hard behind him.

That was all I could take for one day. My head in my hands, I broke into sobs. Damn everything.

When I finally got a grip, I blew my nose and rinsed my face with cold water. Will's words had brought back too much of the past–fleeing through the streets of Baltimore, alone and without family. I'd slept in stalls and stolen food to survive. If racehorse trainer, Jim Ravinski, hadn't taken me under his wing, I might have ended up walking the streets like other homeless runaways.

And now Jim was dead. And me? I'd never fully recovered from the fear and physical damage caused by my fall at Laurel. I could still ride races, but I wasn't the optimistic athlete I'd been before my injuries and Jim's death. Some of the owners and trainers at Laurel Park had stopped putting me on their horses.

Will was right. My greatest desire was to be secure. My greatest fear was that I could become destitute again. The job with the TRPB had been a godsend. Now, it looked like I might lose it. That, and Will's shooting star comment had left me unnerved.

All of this because I wanted to protect him. I still loved Will. I might not be *in love* with him anymore, but I'd do anything to keep him safe.

Glancing at the clock, I saw it was after six. I thought about calling Greta and meeting her somewhere for dinner but couldn't face trying to act normal. I'd save that for the next day. I had to be at the sound stage early and had some script to read.

When I grabbed the hotel phone to call room service, my cell chimed. A shot of fear coursed through me. Was it one of the thugs? Or maybe an angry call from Will?

Seeing Jamie's name on the screen, I went limp with relief. The things that had happened in my hotel room earlier seemed unreal, like a violent scene from a movie. Except, it had been real. Now I didn't know if Jamie or the evil Dillon was on the other end of the incoming call. I'd deal with him tomorrow. I let the call go to voice mail and ordered dinner.

Outside my bedroom window, it was almost dark. My room overlooked the hotel's circular entrance, and I watched as several people walked toward the lobby doors below. The last light from the setting sun reflected from the windows of the cars parked in the hotel lot. Two or three of them were dark SUVs. Of course, they were. I backed away from the glass, pulled the curtains, and turned on some lamps.

Two bourbon and waters later, I wasn't happy, but my nerves had untangled, and dinner arrived. I kept the TV going but have no recollection of watching anything. I hated being afraid, and it was starting to make me mad.

If I wanted to keep my job with the TRPB, I had to find out what was going on at Estrella Studios. Only someone there could have known about my room change.

Gabriel obviously knew who the one-eared man was. Why else would he be so afraid? I'd been told not to discuss any of this with him. But screw that. I was going to talk to him.

Still, I needed to think this through. My phone was bugged, my whereabouts would always be known. Gabriel's phone, undoubtedly, was bugged as well. Hell, they'd probably already planted a listening device in my new room.

The obvious answer was to buy a burner, unless someone was so doggedly tracking me they would be watching me buy one.

The sound stage had enough wires and microphones to supply every criminal in the state of California. I didn't trust my driver or Zalaya as far as I could throw them, but Gabriel was just as afraid as I was. And he *knew* something.

# 18

Riding through the streets of Arcadia the next morning, I longed to call Will and patch things up. No way I could do that, so I stared at the back of my driver's head, wishing I could read his mind. How much did he know? Would he recognize the men who'd come to my room? Did he leak information about me?

He caught me staring in his rear-view mirror. "Is there something I can do for you, Ms. Latrelle?"

"Uh, no. I mean, you're sure they'll have everything I need at the sound stage?"

"Like I told you, Ms. Latrelle, they brought a new wardrobe and makeup trailer to the sound stage last night. You'll be all set, okay?"

"Yeah, sure," I said.

My hands held the sides we'd supposedly use that day. I read my part of the script again, wondering why there was only one scene and why it was so short. The scene was to take place in Dillon's "apartment."

The set up for me being there had been filmed the day before. Millie playing her role as the racehorse owner had wanted to oil the turbulent waters between her two jockeys. She'd met with Dillon at his apartment, then asked me to meet with them both. I'd agreed reluctantly.

An urgent phone call had been written into the script, causing Millie to leave in a rush, thus leaving me alone with Dillon. The sex scene between us was supposed to take place today. I had mixed emotions about this. I didn't want Dillon, but I'd be lying if I said I didn't want Jamie. How could I be interested in sex after having my life threatened? Easy. Being close to death made me giddy just to be alive. It also made me want to grab what I could while there was time.

The Lincoln I rode in drew closer to the sound stage. Even if I wanted to grab some life with my handsome British actor, how could I act natural in front of a camera crew? I was so wired with nerves I was surprised my skin wasn't glowing and twitching.

My mom used to play a Kinks song with the line, "mixed up, muddled up, shook up world." The events of the last few days had left me needing a shrink. Maybe two shrinks. One for Nikki, and one for her character, Fay.

When I'd been hired to play the role of Fay, Zalaya had hooked me up with a film agent who had assured me my contract did not call for nudity. But remembering how rough Jamie as Dillon could be, a twitch of doubt skittered across my spine.

When we arrived at the Estrella sound stage, I scanned the parking lot for the new trailer my driver had mentioned. I didn't see one, only that four of the "star" trailers had been brought in, including the one I'd inherited from Catalina. After dropping our phones off, my driver left me at the sound stage entrance.

Inside, I gaped at a bus-sized RV that must have rolled in through the large bay entrance. A door at the driver's end was open as well as one at the back of the bus. A framed still of Ingrid Bergman from the movie Casablanca hung next to the rear door. Bogart was up by the front one, smoking a cigarette.

I made a beeline for Ingrid and climbed up the steps. The RV was so large that the woman's half had a double-racked wardrobe area, a bathroom with shower and multiple makeup and hair stations.

The makeup artist I'd met before was working on Millie, who gave me a little wave and motioned for me to sit at the station next to her. She didn't speak as her lips were being done. As soon as I perched on the chair, a thin woman with a white-blond buzz cut went to work on me.

When my makeup was done, Pinky handed me a lavender lace bra and matching bikinis, as well as a short black dress with silver buttons down the front. The accessibility provided by the buttons made me nervous. Which is not to say I wasn't already nervous about –– everything.

I stepped into a curtained alcove to change. When I came out Millie was dressed in a sharp looking tweed suit and high heels. I'd been given black and silver heels to match the dress.

"You look adorable, Fay," Millie said.

Still not used to being called Fay, I had to restrain myself from turning around to see who Millie was talking to. But I couldn't control the frantic question that popped from my mouth. "Dillon's not going to rip these buttons off, is he?"

Millie's laugh was as light and bright as a handful of newly minted dimes. "Of course not, but if you think about it, there might be worse things that could happen."

She had no idea how true that was. After having a hideous man hold a knife to my throat, being ravished by Dillon would be a picnic. I forced a smile for Millie, as if she'd made a cute joke.

"Just go with it, Fay. You'll be great."

A radio hooked to Pinky's belt clicked on. When a male voice said, "Ten minutes," I felt like a herd of tiny wild horses was galloping in my stomach.

There was a soft knock on our door, Pinky opened it. A guy from catering handed her a glass of ice and amber liquid. Glancing at me, he said, "Compliments of Mr. Jackson."

Pinky handed me the glass, and the warm scent of expensive whiskey tickled my nostrils. I turned to Millie. "Should I drink this? It's bourbon."

"That's what you always drink, isn't it?"

When I nodded, she said, "Knock it back, kid. It won't hurt you."

So, I did, and the wild horses in my stomach stopped stampeding. It felt more like they were standing around grazing, waiting to see what happened next.

I entered Dillon's "apartment" wearing my black dress with silver buttons. His eyes followed me with a look that said he'd like to have his way with me before he killed me.

Playing her role as racehorse owner, Millie greeted me and encouraged her two jockeys to make peace with each other.

The assistant cameraman was on the rolling platform with the big camera, while Gabriel shot closeups with a thirty-thousand-dollar handheld Canon. He seemed afraid to meet my gaze, a sharp reminder that we'd been told not to speak to each other. Zalaya, on the other hand, was watching everything like a hawk.

Millie began soothing the waters by telling her jockeys she'd bought another grade I stakes winner, the idea being we'd have two good horses to share.

I had to admit it, Jamie Jackson was a damn good actor. He managed to convey with his face that Dillon wanted and intended to ride both horses, even though his lines had him agreeing with Millie's plan. I, on the other hand, playing the role of Fay, was supposed to believe the plan was viable.

Millie received her emergency phone call, rushed off the set, and Dillon took advantage of my guard supposedly being down. He did an excellent portrayal of conning me to believe he was fine with the new arrangement and was happy for me.

Zalaya yelled, "Cut! *No*, no, Fay! It's obvious you don't believe a word Dillon is saying. Do it again, and this time appear more naïve and trusting."

It took two more takes to satisfy Zalaya. And then he had us do a third, which segued into Dillon getting me to sit next to him on his couch. His behavior changed. Suddenly he was sweet and wanting to please me, talking about how great it was we could get along together.

It was hard to act like I believed him, and Zalaya stopped us again. I remembered what Millie had said about choices, and when the camera rolled again, Fay chose to believe Dillon, chose to believe she wanted this incredibly sexy man. The last part, truth be told, was easy.

Dillon leaned in for a kiss. He started slow. I had a nice buzz from the bourbon, and I went with it. Gabriel had the Canon in our faces, catching Dillon's expression as he stopped the kiss and stared into my eyes a moment.

He kissed me again and my body responded. The heat between us built and he did just what I'd known he would. He ripped my dress open. My buttons flew through the air and rolled across the floor, a broken strand of silver pearls. Dillon picked me up, lay me on his bed, put his lips on my neck and a hand on my lace covered breast.

Zalaya yelled, "Cut! That was perfect. Great job you two."

The only problem was Dillon was still on top of Fay and going for broke.

"Get off me," I yelled.

Gabriel rushed over, grabbed Dillon's shoulder and rolled him off me. "Whoa, cowboy," he said, in his French accent.

I snatched the bed sheet over the breast that Dillon had exposed. "You son of a bitch!" I yelled. And then I started giggling. I couldn't help it. The whole situation was ridiculous.

Dillon's mouth twitched as he struggled and failed to stay in character. "Babe, you are so adorable, I got carried away. I'm sorry, but where the hell did you learn to kiss like that?"

"None of your business," I said.

But the way he'd said he was sorry had rung true. Suddenly he was Jamie again. I pulled my dress together and emerged from under the sheet

Millie, who'd watched the scene, said, "Man, the fans are going to *love* this. You two were hot!"

Gabriel puffed up like a rooster ready to crow. "I told you she was right for this movie!"

"That you did," Zalaya replied.

My eyes met Gabriel's. He flinched and looked away. His action jerked me back to the reality of the situation we were in. My fingers started to twist a lock of my hair, an old nervous habit of mine. I made myself stop and turned to Jamie.

"Thanks for sending me that drink."

"I thought it might help."

"It did."

"Listen," he said. "After we film at Santa Anita, I'd like to take you to dinner again, make up for the . . . buttons."

"I think-"

"Time for you jockeys to change," Zalaya said. "The cars will be waiting outside for you and the crew members. We need to get to the track, so move it."

When I entered the RV parked inside the sound stage, Pinky was ironing the dress Millie had worn a day earlier. The trailer smelled of steam and the Dryel cleaner Pinky had used. She did a double take when she saw the tattered state of my black dress. "Looks like Jamie was hot to trot."

Wanting to sidestep the issue, I said, "He's a good actor, and right now I need a set of exercise clothes for the track."

She raised an eyebrow. "Come on, Nikki, give. How was he? Was it fun?"

"So, do you have some exercise clothes or am I supposed to ride in the limo in my underwear?"

"No need to get what's left of your panties in a knot." She went to the clothes rack and moments later I stepped out wearing jeans, boots and a turtle-neck.

Zalaya, Gabriel and some of the crew were watching the monitor on the big camera. They appeared amused as they watched the film and discussed it. Zalaya's lips were curved in a smile as he rubbed his soul patch. Seeing me, he waved.

"We've got some excellent stuff here, Ms. Latrelle."

"That's great," I said, and turned away. I had no intention of standing with them while they stared at me with hardly any clothes on.

I didn't see Dillon. He was probably still in the men's half of the RV, hopefully taking a cold shower.

With a glance to make sure no one was watching me, I slipped through the door to the long hallway that ran down the side of the building. I didn't have much time, but I wanted to check out Zalaya's office. Maybe I'd find something to stop the widening rift between me, Will and my job with the TRPB. Reaching his office door, I turned the handle. It was locked.

Determined to find something, I trotted down the long hall in the opposite direction and found the exit door the thugs must have used the day before. The second thing I discovered creeped me out. There were a lot of mirrors used as décor for the sets inside the sound stage. Apparently, every mirror on the opposite side of this wall was a two-way.

Anyone standing in this hall could watch what was filming on the other side. With a shudder, I realized I was staring into the set of Dillon's bedroom.

Who would do this? Zalaya, as the film's director, and Gabriel, as director of photography were always involved in the filming. So, who had been hiding on the other side watching? The thought of the diamond and gold men watching me through one of these windows, made me sick. And what about the one-eared man?

Even if they were associates of Vos, and I didn't know for sure they were, what possible reason could men like that have for watching the filming of *The Final Furlong?*

I had no idea. The path I'd have to take to find out scared the hell out of me. But suppose I kept quiet, did nothing, and they killed Will anyway? How would I live with that?

# 19

When we reached the track, Dillon, Millie, and I were sent to the parking lot outside the backstretch's main gate. Reddinger was already there, his silver hair and Stetson hat unmistakable.

The sky was slightly overcast, the air on the chilly side, and I was glad Pinky had given me a leather jacket to slip over the turtleneck. A darker cloud scuttled overhead as my gaze wandered toward the base camp. Unwanted images blossomed in my head like poisonous flowers.

*Dave, in his truck, sliding out of sight as gore splattered the passenger window. The photo of his body on a slab in the morgue.*

I shivered violently and fought to clear my head. Breathe, Nikki. breathe. Standing just outside the backstretch barns, I could see and smell the horses. The familiar odors of sweet feed, hay, liniment, and horse accompanied by an occasional whicker or snort created a natural tranquilizer that soothed my anxiety.

I was just beginning to relax when an assistant hustled toward Dillon and me and handed us our sides. Since Millie and Reddinger had more to do in the upcoming scene, they'd received their script before we left the studio. I was grateful that Dillon and I had so few lines, and after a third read, we handed the papers back to the assistant. While we'd been reading, the camera truck and crew had finished setting up.

The scene would feature Millie, Reddinger, and the arrival of the Millie's new "champion" horse, London Fog. I was curious what Stan had chosen and hoped the horse would be as authentic looking and beautiful as the injured Galaxy. After his shoulder had been torn open by the truck's side mirror, Galaxy had been shipped out. Fortunately, Will had found him a good home.

101

A few minutes later, when an eighteen-wheeler horse van rumbled into the lot, Zalaya called for action. With a hiss of air brakes, the big van stopped near the camera truck.

From inside, the slam of a metal horseshoe striking the van's interior wall vibrated through the air. A loud, angry neigh rolled past us. Several horses on the backstretch answered the newcomer's call. I hoped they'd get the horse off the van before he injured himself.

Probably, no one had told London Fog that tantrums were not a part of his script. I glanced at Gabriel and wasn't surprised to see his mouth tight with annoyance. He made an irritated Gallic motion with his hand. Dillon and I exchanged a look and managed keep our faces expressionless.

In the world of expensive racing stock, grooms usually ride in the van with their horses. Since Orlando was a paid Estrella extra, he'd ridden in with London Fog and I could see his face through one of the van's open windows. So did the camera.

The driver climbed down from his cab, opened the van's side door, pulled out the ramp, and set up the wings.

Orlando led the new cast member out while the camera's eye watched. London Fog was big. A handsome dappled gray gelding, with a dark mane and tail, he had a white blaze. I liked his intelligent expression and the proud way he carried himself. I hoped the script called for me to ride him.

Zalaya gave us our cue, and Dillon and I entered the scene where Reddinger and Millie were admiring their new arrival. After we said our lines, Zalaya yelled, "That's a wrap." Dillon and I followed behind London Fog's impressive hindquarters as Orlando led him away from the van.

"He looks sound," I said quietly to Dillon.

"Maybe that wanker, Stan, laid off the Crown Royal long enough to get the right horse this time."

Orlando took London through the gate and up to our barn, where Stan limped from his office to watch the animal's arrival. Greta and Jerry, who were waiting for us, were scheduled to ride on the track with Dillon and me. London Fog, Daisy Dan, Predator, and Mystery Ride were scheduled for the upcoming scene. Mystery Ride was to be Millie's other "champion."

Glancing around the barn area, there was no sign of Will, which seemed odd since the new horse had just come in. I wanted to call him, then remembered a third party could be listening to the conversation. Besides, Will and I were on shaky ground, and the thought of talking to him was just one more thing to be anxious about.

As I drew closer to Stan, I could smell whiskey on his breath. Maybe he needed it for the pain in his leg. More likely he was an alcoholic. Again, I wondered why they had hired this guy to run the barn.

London Fog, now in Galaxy's old stall, thrust his head over his metal gate and whinnied. When I moved closer and put a tentative hand on his neck, he leaned into it, then nodded his head up and down happily when I scratched his chest.

"You're just a big pussy cat," I said. He nodded his head as if in agreement.

"He sure is a looker," Greta said.

"He is," I agreed. "Stan, what do we know about this guy?"

Stan sucked his cheeks in and gave me a narrow-eyed stare. "Don't you worry 'bout him. He'll be all right."

My question had ruffled Stan's feathers, put him on the defensive. Forcing a pleasant smile, I said, "Yeah, you're right, Stan. The horse seems kind and sensible."

Apparently placated, Stan grinned. "He gets his looks from his sire, Ghost Zapper. Only this one here, he never zapped." He laughed loudly, then slurred his next sentence. "His owner was thappy to sell him."

Greta and I exchanged an eyeroll, and Dillon scowled.

Gabriel, who'd been watching us, motioned with his arm to get our attention. "Come on, you guys, let's saddle up and ride. Fay, you're on the new horse. Dillon, you take Mystery Ride."

"Hold on," Zalaya said, waving some sheets of paper. "The four of you need to read these first."

Glancing at the script, I was relieved to see we weren't breaking from the starting gate. I didn't want to depend on a horse, unfamiliar with movie cameras and rolling carts, being calm enough to readily enter the narrow confines of a steel cage.

Maybe Stan had lectured Gabriel about the swiftly changing fight or flight mentality of the average Thoroughbred racehorse. More likely, Gabriel had learned his lesson with Galaxy and Catalina. The guy wasn't stupid.

Or was he? He'd gotten himself mixed up in some weird mess with these thugs and the creep with one ear. And now I was in it too. I realized I was gritting my teeth hard enough to break something. I forced my jaw to relax and went to find the tack for London Fog.

Out on the track, with the camera truck close behind, we rode four abreast, working from a canter into a gallop.

Beyond the inside rail, the sprinkler system was showering the turf track. A breeze sent the smell of wet earth and grass to my nostrils. Above us, a brilliant green Parakeet flashed past. It still surprised me to see these exotic birds flitting among the palms.

Beneath me, the steady, confident rhythm of London's gallop was an additional tonic to my soul. I almost felt normal.

In the movie script, it was supposed to be the day after London Fog's arrival and we were out for morning exercise. Our instructions called for Jamie's Dillon character and me to outdistance Jerry and Greta, to show the superior speed of Millie's two "champions." On the rail near the grandstand another camera was trained on Reddinger as he watched the horses and gripped a stop watch.

At the top of the stretch, Jamie and I put some tension on our reins and asked for speed. Meanwhile, Jerry and Greta pretended to be busy with their whips while actually asking for nothing.

London and Mystery Ride drew well clear and charged toward a second camera truck that filmed a head-on view of us rocketing down the stretch. Jamie and I worked well together, keeping the horses even as if we were in a dead heat. When we flew past Reddinger, he must have clicked his stopwatch for the camera, because in my peripheral vision he was pumping a victorious fist in the air.

By the time we eased to a trot, Gabriel and the main camera truck had caught up with us. Gabriel was all smiles as he called out the window.

"That was perfect. We did it in one take! You guys created a perfect dead heat. Kudos!"

Jamie tipped his riding helmet toward Gabriel and I sketched him a wave, too out of breath for words. The camera truck left us behind, as we slowed our horses to a walk and headed for the pass to the backstretch.

I used my crop to wipe foam from London's neck. He'd produced a lot more sweat than Mystery Ride, and I was truly glad we'd done the scene in one take. The horse wasn't fit enough for a repeat.

"That was brilliant, yeah?"

"Not too shabby," I replied.

"Nice to be out here with someone who can ride."

"Thank you, *Jamie*," I said.

The smile he gave me was a powerful thing. "I guess Dillon's been a little rough on you, yeah?"

"You could say that."

"I meant what I said earlier, Nikki. I want to take you to dinner tonight. Consider it *the revenge of the silver buttons*. We'll drink champagne."

"Veuve Clicquot?"

"Absolutely," he said.

I twined my fingers in London's dark mane. "And you promise to be *Jamie* and not Dillon?"

"Cross my heart."

"Deal," I said.

Once I was back in my room, I fired up my laptop to search London Fog's pedigree and past performances. His grey coloring came from a top sire named Tapit. The stallion currently commanded a $185,000 stud fee.

Curious to know more, I went to Brisnet and looked up London Fog's past performances, surprised to see the horse had earned over $500,000 and won a Grade II stake, going a mile and a quarter at Belmont. His owners must have regretted the fact that the horse was a gelding. He had stamina and speed.

But in his next race, he was vanned off the track, and subsequent X-rays found several chips in his knee. He'd had a long layup and his owners must have felt they'd gotten their money out of him, or believed he'd never be the same horse. They'd sold him to Estrella Studios for an undisclosed amount.

I put the laptop away, and that evening Jamie took me back to the Derby restaurant. We were again seated at a semiprivate corner table, with a crisp white tablecloth, and a small brass lamp. A vase of velvet red roses stood next to the lamp, their scent heady and sweet. They were the only flowers in the restaurant. I suspected Jamie had called ahead.

Not wanting to stare at him, I glanced at the pictures of Sea Biscuit and other champions of long ago. I was pleased to see a new picture hanging of the more recent champion, California Chrome. He was one of my favorites.

American racing fans had been so proud when their 2014 Kentucky Derby winner had shipped half way around the world for the 2015 Dubai World Cup, and finished second. He'd repeated the journey in 2016 and, incredibly, had won! That race had paid just under nine million dollars, and Chrome became one of the top-earning racehorses in history.

"Earth to Nikki," Jamie said. "Are you here or off somewhere with that chestnut horse?"

"Sorry. I was reliving some great American racing history."

"Perhaps this will get your attention," he said as the waiter delivered a bucket of ice and a bottle of Veuve Clicquot.

"Most definitely," I shifted my gaze to meet his.

I'd purposely dressed conservatively. With a loose-fitting black pant suit, a white blouse buttoned almost to my chin, and a minimum of makeup, I was hardly provocative. But the way Jamie was looking at me, I could have been wearing the ripped open black dress and the lavender lace undies.

I stared at my fork and pushed it back and forth nervously. As soon as the champagne was poured, I focused on the bubbles rising in my flute and took a sip. But Jamie was still watching me and his eyes were hungry. It caused a little thrill to flash through me and then head south.

The bubbles weren't the only things rising at our table.

We had lobster and salad with crusty rolls and butter. We drank the whole bottle of champagne and most of a second. After coffee we headed back to the Marriott,

Without protest, I let Jamie take me to his room. I did not want to fall for this guy, but my body wasn't listening. Will was right. I'd wanted Jamie Jackson since the first time I laid eyes on him. I pushed thoughts of Will from my mind and turned to Jamie.

Slowly, he undid my buttons, and then my clothes were off so fast it took my breath away. He was hard and fast, yet somehow as delicate as the roses he'd placed on the table. He heightened my senses until they boiled over and I was left gasping.

But he was more than a good lover, he knew how to make me laugh.

"You drove me *hard* to the finish," he complained as we lay together panting.

"I drove *you*? You were whipping and driving me right over the edge!"

"Yeah, and you hated every minute of it, didn't you?"

I wanted to come up with a clever response, but burst out laughing instead.

Lying on his back, he turned his head toward me, his eyes intense and blue.

"Admit it," he said. "You had to surrender. There's a reason we Brits ruled the world for centuries."

"Here's what you can do with your British invasion," I said, pouncing on top of him with a fierceness that surprised me. Holding his shoulders down, I planted a deep kiss on his lips.

"God save the Queen," he gasped. Then he rolled me over so he was on top, and we started all over again.

# 20

When I woke up in my room the next morning, I was happy and had no regrets. If I'd been a cat, I would have been purring.

My mood lasted through one luxurious stretch. Then my falling out with Will and the events leading up to it came rushing back, dissolving my lazy contentment.

The thugs who'd threatened me had made it clear they wanted me to continue acting. Why did they care about that? Were they that closely associated with Vos? He was an investor in the movie, so of course he wanted to turn a profit. But what was in it for these goons? And why the need to threaten violence? There was a hidden agenda in this thing, and I needed to find out what it was before Will and I ended up on a slab like Dave.

In the shower, I stood beneath a stream of hot water. It did little to ease the cold knot of fear inside me. I dressed in riding clothes since Jamie, Millie and Reddinger were shooting on the sound stage and I was free.

Still, it was a dark, or non-racing day, and as I was still working for Will, or at least I hoped I was, I needed to help get the horses out. It would be good to see Greta and do something routine like riding. But after that? I needed a plan.

I stopped at a Starbucks for breakfast and as the first jolt of caffeine hit me, a woman on crutches was struggling to get inside. I grabbed my breakfast bag and hurried to hold the heavy glass door open for her.

Seeing her brought Catalina to mind. I wondered how she was doing and what she might know. I breathed in the clear air outside Starbucks and climbed into my Toyota. It was time to get to work; screw the thugs.

I had some good gallops on the track with Greta, glad for the opportunity to relax and use my muscles. When I was done, I drove to one of those gas-and-shop places that sells burner phones.

A sudden wave of paranoia hit me. Was someone following me? I drove around the block. Twice. Then I made a fast turn into an alley that went through to the next street before I returned to the store. I didn't see anyone suspicious.

Inside, I was still uneasy. How did I know that the shifty looking guy picking through the energy drinks wasn't there to spy on me, to report I was purchasing a phone?

*Get a grip, Nikki.*

I grabbed a burner with lots of minutes and a charger that would plug into my car. I paid cash for it at the counter, hurried to the Toyota, plugged in the phone to charge, and repeated my round the block and through the alley procedure.

I drove to the hospital and hurried inside to the section where Catalina had been. At the nurse's station, a Miss Espinosa told me Catalina had been moved to a new location where she could receive physical therapy.

"That's why I'm here," I lied. "She told me the name, and I wrote it down, but I've lost the piece of paper. How dumb is that? Can you remind me where she went?"

Looking at me carefully, Espinosa asked, "Are you a relative?"

"Yes, I'm her sister, but I've been out of town and feel terrible that I didn't have time to see her until today."

Thank God the man's name came to me, and without a break, I continued on. "I did talk to Doctor Chen when Catalina was first injured, but like I said, I got called out of town. I just got back, and I'm praying you can give me the name of the place. I really want to see how she's doing. She'll kill me if she knows I'm back and didn't bother to see her. She–

Espinosa raised her hand. "Stop! I'll give you the name, already."

She clicked some keys on her computer. "She's at the Monrovia Canyon Spa and Rehabilitation facility."

She wrote the name on a piece of paper along with the address and phone number. Ripping the note off the gummed pad, she said, "See if you can manage not to lose this."

"Oh, I won't," I said with my best fake smile, but the woman had turned away from me. Sometimes, if you drive people crazy, they'll do anything just to get rid of you.

My thug supplied iPhone had a terrific GPS app on it, but I didn't want anyone to know I was visiting Catalina. The burner had limited ability, but it seemed like it would be able to get me to Monrovia Canyon. From there, I could ask.

I hadn't realized how quickly the road would rise to the Santa Gabriel Mountains. In less than six miles, I had reached the Monrovia Canyon area and was surrounded by steep, rocky hills, and a heavy growth of evergreen trees and bushes. I kept going until I found a gas station where I asked for directions to the Monrovia facility. Ten minutes later, I entered through stone gates and cruised along a beautifully planted drive. The scent of eucalyptus and flowers wafted through my open window.

I parked before a handsome stone building with a terracotta roof and tall, sparkling windows. Estrella Studios had spared no expense for Catalina. Or maybe Julio Vos really was her uncle, and he'd sprung for the expense.

Inside, I told the well-coiffed, smartly-dressed woman behind the counter I was a friend of Catalina's and hoped to visit her. The woman's discreet badge indicated her name was Betty, and Betty was looking askance at my riding clothes and dusty boots.

I gave her what I hoped was an apologetic smile. "Sorry about my outfit, but I just came from the racetrack where Catalina was working with me when she got hurt."

Betty digested this, nodded, then smiled. "Oh, okay. I'm glad you came. She hasn't had any visitors except her uncle, Mr. Vos. I'm sure she'll be delighted to see you."

I wasn't sure about it at all.

Betty picked up her desk phone and asked for someone to come to the front desk to escort a visitor.

A male nurse led me down a terrazzo hallway with a bank of tall windows and potted palms on one side and rocking chairs on the other. The chair's cushions were a pretty green-and-pink palm print, but no one was rocking. With a right turn we entered a section with rooms for the patients.

Stopping at a doorway, he said, "She's in here." He stepped into the room, "Catalina, you have a visitor."

She was stretched out on one of those beds with multiple settings. The end beneath her head was raised and another hump appeared in the middle to support her leg, which was in a cast.

She had a nasty looking metal brace around her neck. It contrasted sharply with the flouncy floral pillows beneath her head, a matching bedspread, and silky aqua bed-skirt that draped to the floor.

The room had a tall window with yet another potted palm and rocking chair. A white bureau with an elegant, scalloped mirror completed the decor. The place must cost a fortune.

"Did you come here to stare at me, Nikki, or do you have something to say?"

The same hard Catalina.

"Sorry," I said. "I just feel so bad for you. Are you in much pain?"

"What do *you* think?" Her question dripped with sarcasm.

She looked miserable. Her face was almost gray, and lines from the agony she'd endured since her fall were etched into her skin.

Moving closer to the bed, I asked "May I sit with you?"

"Whatever."

Not much of an invitation, but I perched carefully on the edge of her bed near her hand. Her fingers picked at the spread. When I gently covered her hand with mine, her upper lip buckled and tears welled in her eyes.

"Why are you being so nice to me?" A sudden storm of emotion broke the dam and she started sobbing.

"You've been through hell," I said. "Someone should be nice to you."

"But I treated you like shit."

"I think you were just scared," I said. A white table by the headboard held a gold box of tissues. I grabbed a handful, and she took them.

"It was that obvious?"

"Kind of," I said. "Did you really ride in races in Mexico?"

"No, it was a lie Uncle Julio made up. I know how to ride, but I was never a jockey."

I was slightly shocked by her admission. But she was still crying, as if the dam that had broken had released all the lies.

"He told me he was involved in this movie, and that Jamie Jackson would be one of the stars. I begged him to get me a part."

I bet she did. "But," I said, "the part was a little more than you bargained for?"

"It's been *awful*. I thought it would be easy. And now this." She lifted one hand toward her neck and pointed at her broken leg.

"I'm really sorry this happened to you," I said.

"Yeah, me too."

Her voice had grown steadier. The worst of the storm over.

I stared at the window. The sun had worked its way through the window's plantation shutters, throwing dappled light onto the potted palms leaves.

"You know," I said, handing Catalina another tissue so she could finish mopping up. "I was in a terrible fall a couple of years ago. It really messed me up. Took me months to recover and to be honest with you, I haven't been the same since."

"You're afraid?"

I could feel my lips press into a grimace. "It's more like I've lost the will to win at all costs."

We were both silent a minute and it seemed as good a time as any to do a little prying.

"So, your Uncle Julio is an investor in *The Final Furlong?*"

"Yes."

"I guess he's been involved in the movies before?"

"No. This is the first one. Some people he knows got him involved."

I remembered the flash drive with the video of Zalaya talking to the one-eared man, the one that had resulted in Dave's death.

"So, I guess your uncle knows some movie people."

"No, I don't think they're movie people. I've never met them, but as far as I know they don't have a background in film."

So, what the hell did they have a background in? "They must be involved somehow. Your uncle never said?"

Catalina's eyes narrowed. "No, and why are you so interested, anyway?"

I gave a little shoulder shrug and did some back pedaling. "Just curious how all this works. I mean it's so interesting, right? Movie stars, film companies, the green screen stuff. It's pretty cool."

"It *was*," she said. "Now I don't care if I never see another camera. Look, Nikki. I appreciate your coming by, but I'm tired and I have therapy soon. Learning to walk again with this thing on my neck is not fun."

"I understand." I rose from my perch on the edge of her bed. "Anything I can get you before I leave?"

"No."

"Hey," I said. "I think I saw your uncle with some Latino guys one day. Are they the people who brought him into the movie?"

She frowned. "I told you, I don't know anything about any of that, so why keep asking me?"

"Just curious, I guess. Well, feel better. I'll stop by again."

"That won't be necessary." The words were sharp and fast.

I gave her a fake smile, said goodbye, and left.

Suddenly I wondered if the Latino thugs didn't work for Vos. Maybe he worked for them.

# 21

On the way back to Arcadia, the phone the thugs gave me dinged with a text from Gabriel. "Your driver will pick you up at 7:00 a.m. tomorrow. You're due on set at eight."

I texted that I'd be ready. A few minutes later I heard the ring of an incoming call.

It was Jamie, and I answered.

"Nikki, I just escaped the studio. I had trouble focusing. Couldn't stop thinking about you and last night, could I? Please tell me you're free for dinner."

The sound of his voice hit me with an electric shock of anticipation. I was almost too happy to hear from him. But with all the weird stuff that had been going on, so what if I was sliding into what was likely a pointless affair? Jamie had thrown me a lifeline, and I intended to grab it.

"What time?" I asked.

"We have to be on set early tomorrow. How about 5:30?"

"See you then," I said." I was glad it was only three in the afternoon. I needed some alone time in my hotel room.

As I pulled into the Marriott's parking lot, I got another call. The screen indicated it was Will. I was nervous about talking to him, especially on a bugged phone. I let him go to voice mail. I could have called him back from my burner, but his own phone might be as compromised as my iPhone.

In my room, housekeeping had made my bed and straightened up the mess of stuff I'd left on the desk. They'd left fresh towels in the bathroom, and a short time later, I used one to dry off after a hot shower.

I pulled on some designer jeans that had silver zippers at the ankles and a matching denim jacket. Pinky had given me the outfit saying they'd already been used in a film and she thought they'd fit me. I've never been a trendy dresser, but I had to admit the combo looked cute. I was starting to like these movie perks.

Thinking of Jamie, I fluffed my hair, and applied some makeup. I was admiring myself in the mirror when there was a hard knock on the door. I froze. Thoughts of Jamie flew from my mind, replaced by an image of the one-eared man and his knife. Or the Latino thugs and their guns.

The knock came again, only it was more like pounding. I'd stopped breathing. Fear kept me away from the door's peep hole.

"Nikki, open up!" It was Will's voice. The sudden relief almost made me dizzy.

"Jeez," I said, opening the door. "Do you have to sound like a SWAT team on a raid? You scared me." He had no clue how much.

Stalking into the room, he grabbed my arm as he passed me, spinning me around to face him. "Look, Nik, you work for me and I'd appreciate your answering the phone when I call. You don't even bother to call me back."

When I stared at his hand that gripped my arm, he dropped it and I took a step back.

"I'm sorry" I said. "I was asleep earlier."

"Bullshit, Nikki. Your car engine's still warm. You gonna tell me you lent your car to someone while you were napping?"

I tried to think of a response and failed.

Will stared at me with cold eyes. He shook his head, his lip curled in disgust. He had never looked at me like that before. It hurt.

He turned away and paced across the room. When he passed the desk that held a bunch of my stuff, he stiffened. Slowly, he reached out and picked up a photo.

"What the fuck is this, Nikki?"

I could feel my mouth drop open. He was holding the morgue photo of Dave. The maid must have found it when she plumped the couch cushions. How could I have been so stupid to leave it where someone could find it?

"It's Dave," I mumbled.

"I can see that. What the hell are you doing with it? How did you get this?"

"Um, it just sort of showed up."

"Showed up?"

As he stared at me, some of the anger seemed to leave him. His eyes softened. "Nikki, is someone threatening you?"

I wanted to scream, "Yes! I'm scared and I need help!" But my room was bugged and I still loved Will. I didn't want him to die, so I said nothing.

His lips tightened. "If there's one thing I know about you, Nikki, it's that you're not a coward. So, what's really going on? Is the studio paying you to keep quiet about Dave's murder?"

"No. Nothing's going on." I was pretty sure my poker face had deserted me. I probably looked as miserable as I felt.

Suddenly, he threw his hands up. "You know what? As far as the TRPB is concerned, you're fired! That's it. I'm telling the office to send you your last check and termination notice. I want nothing more to do with you, Latrelle."

Still holding the photo, he marched past me, knocking me out of his way as he went by. Before the door slammed behind him, he waved the picture at me. "Detective Garcia will be asking you about this."

I was too shocked to move. I wanted to run after him, but what could I say? I stumbled to my bed and sat on the edge. My face dropped into hands that were shaking.

I'd lost my job. The movie would end, and I'd be struggling for income again. Worst of all, I'd lost Will. Somehow, I had to fix this.

I put on the best face possible when Jamie picked me up for dinner.

Still, with a questioning look, he said, "You look like you could use a drink."

"I think I could."

"So, what's up?" he asked.

When I answered with a shrug, he grinned. "You missed me that much, yeah?"

"You wish," I said, and flashed him a smile that was real.

We climbed into his convertible Porsche and headed up into the mountains towards a place called Hidden Springs.

His interest in me, along with that stunning face and bright smile, were a tonic. A much-needed break from the stress. It was a good bet that an evening with him could renew my energy and allow me to think more clearly.

The restaurant was high up in the hills. We sat on a terrace overlooking a spectacular view of the dark green redwood forest. Below, I caught glimpses of the waters of Hidden Springs.

When our twenty-something waitress arrived, she had trouble keeping her eyes off Jamie. Blushing, she asked, "Excuse me, but are you Jamie Jackson?"

He gave her his movie star smile. "I am, Laura."

I realized he'd read her name badge. Using her name left Laura all aflutter and no doubt, a fan for life.

"Could you," he asked, "bring my friend here a Wild Turkey 101?" When she nodded, he said, "Make it a double, would you?"

She nodded, and immediately rushed off to get my drink.

"Uh, Laura," he called after her. "I'll have the same."

"Oh! I'm sorry. Yes, of course," she stammered.

"Does this happen often?" I asked.

"Enough that you get used to it. And you should be prepared, because after this movie hits the theatres and streaming services, it will happen to you." He cocked his head to one side, studying me. "A lot."

"I don't think so."

"You underestimate yourself. With those blue eyes, full lips and that fit body, you're the whole package. At least for me you are."

His words left me wondering and uncomfortable. Was that just Hollywood flattery or did he really mean it? "Gee," I said, trying to lighten the mood, "maybe we should get a room."

He lifted the edge of the white tablecloth. "We could duck under here."

Laura was coming with our drinks. "Nah," I said, "Laura might crawl under there with us."

We exchanged grins, and I watched Laura trying not to stare at Jamie while she set our drinks on the table.

Two excellent meals, one bottle of champagne, and a shared tiramisu later, we left the restaurant and drove back to our hotel. In his room, Jamie surprised me. I could see the desire in his eyes, but he held back.

"Nikki, what's eating you?"

This guy paid more attention than I realized. I was quiet a beat before answering.

"Will and I had a fight," I said.

"About what?"

Obviously, I couldn't answer with the truth. I didn't know this man well enough to trust him to keep my secrets.

"I think Will didn't realize how much of my time the movie would take," I said.

"He may be a bit jealous, too. You two used to have a thing, right?"

"Yeah, but it's been over a long time."

"Good to know," he said.

The hunger in his eyes seemed to swallow me. Seconds later, the sparks ignited. Our searching hands and lips produced flames that almost burned my skin. Later, when we finally collapsed, panting, I floated in a delicious afterglow.

# 22

I awoke suddenly at 4:00 a.m. with a loop tape of my fight with Will running in my head. Jamie was asleep, with one muscular leg draped over my thigh. Feeling restless and uneasy, I managed to slip out from under his leg without waking him.

Gathering my clothes from where they were scattered on the floor, I crept into the bathroom, got dressed, and slipped silently into the hall. As I walked to my own room, I agonized over how to fix the danger Will and I were in. I wouldn't get anything more out of Catalina. Questioning Vos would be suicidal.

I had to talk to Gabriel. The goons might have forbidden it, but I didn't care anymore. Gabriel knew more about what was going on and he was as scared as I was. It was idiotic for us not to join forces––whether he wanted to or not.

After changing into clothes to wear to the sound stage, I walked to a nearby twenty-four-hour coffee shop. Two cappuccinos and one toasted bagel later, I got into my car, licking cream cheese off my fingers. Driving to an all-night gas-and-shop, I bought a second burner. For Gabriel.

Then I bought six sim card kits for a buck apiece. I wanted to keep the phones untraceable. And they would be as long as we ripped out each card soon enough, then tossed it. Back in my room, I plugged in the new burner. While it was charging, I lay on the bed to think.

I needed to break into the locked office in the sound stage. I wasn't sure how I'd do it, but knew I needed to go through Zalaya's files. I believed in the axiom "follow the money." If something illegal was going on with the film, no doubt, it would be about money and there may well be a record in that office.

By now, the sun was rising, and my driver would be picking me up soon. I stuffed both my burner phones, pen, small pad of paper, and my wallet in the

Frye leather tote I'd picked up with my first studio paycheck. I'd always wanted one, but had never been able to afford it.

The way things were going, my future would probably be limited to vinyl. After what I intended to say to Gabriel, I'd probably be fired. Again.

We began filming with a scene that was uncannily similar to the early hours of that day. I lay, all but naked, under the covers of the bed in Dillon's "apartment." Our clothes were scattered on the floor, including the buttonless little black dress and lavender lace underwear. It was supposed to be the following morning after Dillon had seduced me.

Naked, he climbed from the bed. I knew they were filming him from his face to just low enough. He was naked because they wanted to shoot a full back view when he turned away from the camera. I could almost hear the unrestrainable gasps of a million female movie fans as they saw his gorgeous, tight butt.

He picked up a long sweatshirt from the back of a chair and threw it at me. "Play time's over, Fay. Put this on. I have to get out of here. Which means, you too."

Following my sides, I scowled at him. "Are you always such a bastard the morning after?"

"Sorry, love, I've got a schedule to meet." Gabriel came in close with the handheld camera, focusing on Dillon's face. Dillon let his expression soften. "I'll make it up to you. Take you to dinner tonight?"

While the camera had been on Dillon, I'd gratefully pulled the sweatshirt over my head, pleased that it was knee length. When Gabriel turned the camera back to me, I gave what I hoped was a cautious smile, playing the role of a woman who was attracted to a bad boy in spite of knowing better.

"Sure, why not?"

Had art ever imitated life more closely? It was creeping me out.

Later that afternoon, after completing a scene with Millie and Reddinger, I was done for the day. But I didn't leave. I planned to wait until everyone was finished then, corner Gabriel.

I watched as Millie and Dillon concluded their scene. Millie made it obvious she was very attracted to Dillon. Any viewer would see Dillon used his sexuality to get what he wanted. I wasn't privy to the script, but I sure hoped in the end, Fay would come to her senses and leave Dillon in her dust during and after the big race scene.

When filming was done, I changed quickly back into street clothes in the big trailer. Then I went to look for Gabriel. I found him with Zalaya reviewing the day's filming in the theatre off the side hall. The last time I'd been in that room, I'd found the flash drive containing Dave's video of Zalaya talking to the one-eared man. Then, Gabriel had thrown me out. We hadn't spoken since.

I sent the two men a bright smile. "Hey, okay if I watch too?"

Gabriel's mouth tightened, but before he could speak, Zalaya, said, "Of course, Nikki. Come on in."

I did and made myself comfortable in one of the big La-Z-Boys. "This theatre is so cool. So, did I do okay today?"

"Better than okay," Zalaya said. "The love-hate thing between you and Dillon is palpable."

"Thanks," I said. "Gabriel, are you pleased with how your filming's going?"

"Yes."

Zalaya stared at Gabriel. "What has gotten in to you? Your work has been spectacular, but you've been edgy for days."

"*Nothing!*" Gabriel's response was overly sharp. After a beat, he said, "Sorry, probably just production stress."

"What stress?" Zalaya asked. "Everything's on schedule, your work is excellent. Maybe you should drink more of your champagne. Bubble yourself up a bit." He snorted a laugh like he'd made a great joke.

Gabriel wasn't smiling. My proximity had shut him down. Too bad.

I noticed that two sets of keys were on the table with Zalaya's other stuff. One was a big ring with his car keys and what must be keys related to the sound stage. There was a small ring with two other tagged keys, but they were too far away to read.

"Here, Nikki," Zalaya said. "This is the scene of you and Dillon."

And once again, there I was in bed with Dillon. But as I'd hoped, I'd been off camera while emerging from under the covers and whipping the sweatshirt over my head.

I sat and watched the rest of the day's films, listening to the two men critique the scenes. With only one more scene to review, Zalaya took a bathroom break. I stood. Stretching and yawning, I walked to the table with the keys. I read the tags on the smaller set. One said "office" and when Gabriel wasn't looking, I palmed them.

When I sat again, Gabriel threw me a scowl that clearly said, "Get out!" Truth be told, he'd given me that look several times.

But Zalaya had ignored him and was just egotistical enough to believe I was there to soak up his brilliant comments. When he returned, he and Gabriel finished their discussion. When Zalaya suggested the three of us go out for a drink, we declined his offer.

I held by breath when Zalaya began to gather his things to leave.

"Where are my office keys? They were right here on this table with these other ones."

"I didn't really notice them," Gabriel said. "Maybe you misplaced them."

"I didn't see them either." I was such a liar. I could feel the metal outline of the keys pressing against my thigh from the inside of my jeans pocket.

"I suppose I could have left them somewhere else."

"Don't you have spares on the big key ring?" Gabriel asked.

"Yes, but–"

"Then don't worry about it," Gabriel said with a shrug. "They'll turn up."

Zalaya scowled. "They'd better."

When Zalaya gave up on the keys, Gabriel stood to make his own exit. I grabbed his sleeve when Zalaya wasn't looking and mouthed, "I have to talk to you."

He shook his head and tried to pull away. I held on with an iron claw, but made sure to smile.

"Zalaya," I said, "I'll see you tomorrow. Gabriel promised me he'd teach me a little about that handheld Canon. It's so *cool* the way he uses it for close work!" I was bubbling with so much enthusiasm, I felt like slapping myself.

"Good idea," Zalaya said. "See you guys tomorrow."

I almost sagged with relief when he left the theatre. I whipped my pen and paper from my tote bag and wrote, "We *have* to talk. I bought you a burner phone." I showed him the note and pulled his phone out of my tote bag and handed it to him with three sim card kits.

Then I wrote, "This place is probably bugged."

Gabriel read the last note and said, "Of course it is."

In as nonchalant tone as I could muster, I said, "Let's take the Canon outside. I'd love to see how it works in the daylight as opposed to the studio lights."

If looks could kill, I would have dropped dead right there in the theatre. Gabriel's lips were so tight with anger, I was afraid he'd hit me. "What the hell do you think you're-"

With a warning glance, I placed a finger to his lips, stopping his outburst.

"Come on," I said. "You promised you'd give me a short lesson. And if not now, when?"

Muttering in French, he put the phone and cards in his carryall and picked up the Canon. I ripped my note into shreds, stuffed them in my tote, and followed him out of the sound stage.

At either end of the parking lot, a bench stood before the hedge that screened the chain link fence. "Let's sit over there," I said, pointing at one.

"You," he said, "are an *imbécile!* Why do you do this? They won't just kill you; they will torture you! Arjun is a sadist."

"Arjun? Is he the man with one ear?"

Gabriel shuddered. "*Oui.* I have witnessed things I will not talk about."

We both glanced around the parking lot like frightened rabbits. I didn't see anyone. The day had been warm and the scent of tar rose from the parking lot's new asphalt. Traffic rushed past us, unseen beyond the hedge. I wanted to be one of those people rushing through a typical day, instead of a nightmare.

"Gabriel, if he and those other two are as bad as you say, why haven't they killed us?"

"They want the movie to stay in production."

"But why?" I asked. "Why do they care so much about the movie?"

"I don't know. I don't want to know."

"So why don't you run, Gabriel?"

"This is my first movie as Director of Photography. If I walk out, it would be almost impossible to get another job. I need this job! And, if you're so smart, why don't *you* leave?"

"I need the money."

Gabriel spread his hands palms up. "So, there you go. Always it is about the money."

I tried again. "Gabriel, we need to find out what's going on. Find a way to protect ourselves. To do that, I need your help."

"Forget it. I am not interested in joining your little mission of suicide."

I pulled my iPhone from my tote. "Do you want me to call and ask for your help on this phone they've bugged?"

His face seemed to crumple. "No, no, no!" His words came out as a wail. His hands covered his face. Tears slid down from beneath them.

I felt like a heartless bitch. "Please, Gabriel, I only need you to help me with one thing. It won't even be dangerous for you. I promise."

His shoulders slumped. His hands dropped from his face. "What is it you want me to do?"

I took a deep breath and told him.

# 23

I'd almost finished telling Gabriel what I needed, when motion at the gate made me pause. My limo was pulling in, so my last words to Gabriel became a galloping paragraph.

I caught my breath, then smiled for the benefit of my driver. Gabriel and I were just two buddies having a good time.

"Pretend you're showing me the camera!"

Gabriel was quick on the uptake, placing my hand on the Canon, pointing at some switches. "Put your eye on the viewfinder. Now, pan the parking lot like you're filming it."

Seeing me in the corner of the lot, my driver steered the Town Car close to us, stopped, and slid his window down.

I did the bubbly voice again. "Thank you, Gabriel. I always wanted to know how to work one of these things! You'd make a great instructor!" Gesturing at the car, I handed the Canon back to Gabriel. "My ride's here. Thanks again."

I climbed into the limo and on the way to the hotel, forced myself to make small talk with the driver. Halfway to the Marriott, Jamie called. As I answered, I had to remind myself to relax. My conversations with Jamie never ventured into the realm of my darker problems.

In fact, our affair, or whatever it was, was an excellent cover. It would keep the thugs thinking Jamie and the film were my primary interests. They didn't need to know I've always been a first-class snoop.

"Nikki, where would you like to have dinner tonight?" He sounded so happy and relaxed. So wonderfully normal.

"Sorry, I have to beg off, Jamie. I think I might have a tummy virus, and you don't want to share *that*."

"Probably not," he said.

I could hear a smile in his voice and liked him for it. He was not one to easily take offense.

"I'll probably be fine by tomorrow night. Can I have a raincheck?"

"You can have whatever you want."

That voice and the promise it held left me with a pang of desire and disappointment. But I needed to focus on the evening ahead and ended the call.

By now we were pulling up before the hotel. As I started to enter the lobby, I noticed a panel truck parked off to the side. I did a double take and stopped. "Larry the Locksmith" was painted on its side. It's not like I was a thief trained in the art of lock picking, but I'd learned a few things when I was on the streets in Baltimore.

"Larry" was in the driver's seat. His door was open and he was talking on his cell. The rear panel doors were wide open, revealing a lovely array of tools.

Once my driver's car disappeared down the street, I hot footed it over to the back of Larry's truck and looked inside. With a quick glance to make sure no one was watching, I grabbed two slender pieces of metal, a small hammer, and slid them in my tote.

Then I made fast tracks through the lobby, took the elevator to my floor, but walked past my room. Seeing no one around, I slipped through the fire door into the staircase, and walked down to the garage level.

I would wait there for Gabriel. Since he was also a guest at the Marriott, anyone watching him, would think it logical he'd use the underground parking.

After ten minutes passed, I became nervous that he might be a no-show. When anyone else drove in or out, I pretended to be talking on my iPhone.

With relief, I heard the little Volkswagen engine, then saw the red convertible. Gabriel parked in an empty spot, climbed out, and looked around with nervous eyes. His usually carefully groomed hair was in disarray.

He waited until there was no sound of a car engine entering or leaving the garage before waving me over. As I hurried to him, he popped open the trunk lid. I had to squeeze into the fetal position to fit in the tiny space. If I wasn't skinny, I couldn't have done it.

Riding in the dark, uncomfortable box, I prayed I hadn't made a mistake about Gabriel. That he wouldn't betray me. I imagined the trunk lid opening only to find Arjun and the two thugs staring down at me.

I fought to get a grip on my nerves. When we finally stopped, and the trunk lid popped open, I exhaled a tightly held breath to see Gabriel above me. He gave me a hand and helped me out. We were inside the sound stage, and he'd parked the little Beetle on the far side of the big studio trailer. The gate guard would never know I was there.

Still, I prayed, if there were surveillance cameras placed inside the studio, no one offsite was monitoring them. I'd never seen a security camera inside, but they could be cleverly hidden.

As far as outside cameras went, almost every time my driver had stopped at the gate, I'd peered into the guardhouse. I'd never seen the monitors in there showing anything but various views of the parking lot and outside fence. Apparently, Estrella's security was only about keeping the public out.

We both stood still listening. The only sound was the humming of the HVAC system.

"There were no cars in the lot, right?" I whispered close to his ear.

"I told you I wouldn't even come in here if there were. Now that I've brought you here, do you want to tell me how you propose to get into Zalaya's office?" He'd asked so quietly I'd barely been able to hear him. Better safe than sorry.

A grin escaped me, and Gabriel's eyes narrowed. "You took his keys, didn't you?"

"Of course, I did. It's not like we want to blow up the office door, is it?" I was starting to do that British thing of ending my sentences in a question. Like Jamie.

I pulled the small key ring from my jeans and we headed for the long side hall to reach Zalaya's office. We arrived at the door, and the key tagged "office" slid easily into the lock. When the door opened, though I knew no one would be there, I was still relieved to find the room empty. Gabriel started to follow me inside, but I held up a hand.

"You've got your burner phone, right?"

He held it up.

"Good, you need to stand watch, Gabriel. Maybe the best way would be to cruise the hall and keep checking the two-way mirrors?"

He nodded, knowing he could see the whole sound stage through the glass

"If anyone comes," I said, "ring my phone once. I'll meet you at your car."

"If you can get that far without getting caught," he said. "I don't like this. It is very foolish to be here at all!"

Gabriel's fear was growing. I tried to buck him up. "Keep the faith, *mon amie*. We'll be out of here *rapidement*."

"We'd better be! And your French accent is terrible."

At least I'd gotten a smile out of him. I tried to keep a calm demeanor but my insides felt like they were crawling with snakes.

As he left for the hall, I turned to inspect the office. There was no window, but a huge photo shot from an airplane covered one wall. It showed the race track with text identifying the names of buildings, barns, and pathways. The photo map outlined where the studio crew was allowed, the location of the base camp and so on. The print brightened one wall with the gold of sunlight, the multiple green shades of eucalyptus, palms, and the barns. The flowers that so many of the trainers hung in their shedrows added splashes of bright color. Almost as good as a window.

Zalaya's large desk was a modern style made of bleached wood and stainless steel. Probably cost a fortune. I pulled a drawer out about six inches and leaned over to look inside. Quietly, it rolled itself closed again. Nice feature if you could pay for it.

Time to stop admiring the furniture and search already. Coming from a have-not background, I'd wasted too much time obsessing over what the "haves" had.

None of the desk drawers were locked, so instead of pawing through them, my gaze settled on a large bleached wood cabinet. The outer door swung out, revealing file drawers inside. Two of them were locked.

Mentally thanking Larry, the Locksmith, I pulled the slender pieces of metal from my tote. The smaller one fit nicely into the key hole of the file drawer, sliding all the way to the tumblers. Hoping I'd get lucky, I tapped the end a few times with the hammer, and twisted. The lock popped open, and I had to restrain myself from dancing a little jig.

Inside there were files marked caterers, carpenters, wardrobe, makeup—all the different people that made up the costs of production. The first thing I looked at were "actors." There was a file on me with a column listing the $32,000 I was being paid. Another column next to it showed a larger sum. No way I was making $45,000 for my role in this film! My contract showed an upper limit of $40,000.

Staring at the page, it hit me like a runaway horse. Zalaya was skimming money off Estrella Studios. I grabbed Gabriel's file. He had two columns as well. I pulled his contract. It showed his pay was capped at $5,000 a week. Zalaya's second column showed him earning $8,000 a week. Zalaya was a crook, but it would probably take a forensic accountant to trace the money.

Interestingly, I saw that Catalina's pay amount had not been tampered with. Zalaya had obviously been afraid of alerting her uncle, Vos. Was Zalaya working for Arjun? I didn't think so. He'd been too frightened when he'd seen Arjun's two thugs with their gold ring and necklace that first night outside the sound stage. The man was playing a dangerous game.

It was so frustrating not to be able to take photos of the papers in Zalaya's file. I cursed the burner phone for not having a camera, but even if I hadn't had to leave the iPhone at the security gate, the pictures would go straight to the thugs, wouldn't they?

I'd found out a lot, but I still didn't know what was up with Arjun, and if he, not Zalaya, was the one who was threatening us. Gabriel poked his head through the door. His forehead was beaded with sweat.

"Nikki, we need to get out of here."

"Has someone come?"

"No, but I can't take this! We need to leave."

"I've got some really interesting stuff to tell you when we get back, Gabriel. Just give me five minutes to see what's in this other file drawer."

He rolled his eyes, and muttered something in French, before saying, "Just hurry!"

"Okay, okay," I said, picking up my slender pick and the hammer. "Keep a look out."

He growled something unintelligible and retreated to the hall.

As I slid the metal in to the second drawer's key hole, I heard a gasp outside the office. Gabriel, white faced and wide eyed, appeared in the doorway.

"Someone's coming!"

I pulled the pick out, grabbed the hammer and stuffed them both in my tote bag. Then I ran after Gabriel who was already racing for his car in the bay where he'd parked it. I hoped he was doing the right thing, that we weren't about to run into the diamond and gold guys.

I caught up to him as he opened the Volkswagen's trunk. "Where are they?" I whispered.

"They parked outside. We're lucky, they're using the entrance door. Get in!" he said, shoving me into the trunk. He closed the lid on me.

I hoped we hadn't been watched through a hidden sound stage security camera. I didn't want to think what could happen if we had.

I heard voices outside the car, and stopped breathing. My jaw was tight enough to crack. When they came closer, I recognized the Latino accents of the two thugs.

"You're here somewhat late, Mr. Dubois. What's going on?"

"My work is never done. If you knew anything about shooting film, you wouldn't have to ask. I've been in the theatre going over some of today's footage."

I was amazed how calm and professional Gabriel sounded. Slowly, I exhaled and forced myself to breathe in again.

"But," Gabriel said, "you're right, it's late, and I need to get to my hotel and sleep. My days start early."

"Of course," a Latino voice said. "You know we expect a great film. It's what Arjun wants."

"Then I'm off," Gabriel said. *"Bonne nuit."*

Again, I wondered why these people were so concerned that the film be successful. It's not like Vos was the only investor, was it? Surely there were others. Not being able to talk to Will and get the answers to these questions was driving me crazy.

The car started, and I allowed myself a long, ragged breath, knowing the engine noise would cover the sound. The car lurched forward, and the tension in my shoulders and jaw began to ease. When I heard us passing through the security gate, I knew we'd made it.

# 24

The next day, being a dark day, Gabriel and Zalaya planned to film us "racing" on the track. As usual there was no need to arrive for wardrobe before 8:30 or nine.

At 7:30, there was a soft knock on my door. My stomach tightened right up, and after a steadying breath, I climbed from beneath the covers, padded to the door and looked through the peep hole. Jamie, holding two large takeout cups from the coffee shop.

When I opened the door, he said, "How's your tummy this morning? Can you handle a cappuccino?"

I almost asked him what he was talking about before remembering I'd begged off the previous evening complaining about a stomach virus. "I slept really well. I feel fine. Thanks," I said, taking a cup from him.

We perched on the edge of my bed, my first sip going down with a sigh of pleasure.

Jamie's blue eyes narrowed. "Watch the sound effects, Nikki, or you're going to get more than just coffee."

I scooted to the side, putting a little distance between us.

"You still on for tonight?" he asked.

When I nodded, he smiled. "Good, because I can't seem to get enough of you."

*Yeah, until the movie's over.*

I squashed the negative thought. "We'll work on that later," I said. "Now, I've got sides to read, and my driver will be here before long."

He drained his cappuccino. "See you on the set, babe."

As soon as he left, I grabbed my cellphone and looked to see if there was a hardware store nearby. There was, only two blocks away. I called their number and learned they opened at eight.

Zipping into the bathroom, I got ready for the day, then headed out the door. It was 7:55 when I trotted to the elevator, out through the lobby, and down the street. I was at the hardware store a few minutes after eight. I gave Zalaya's keys to the man at the duplicating machine, and walked out of the store minutes later with two sets of keys.

A fast trot got me back to the hotel before my driver arrived, and safely in the lobby, where I waited for my limousine.

Out on the track, with the Santa Gabriel Mountains looming in the distance, I jogged the beautiful gray, London Fog. Greta was on Daisy Dan, Jerry on Predator and Jamie on the dark bay "champion," Mystery Ride. Jamie and I both wore Millie's turquoise and purple silks. Wardrobe had put a cute little purple pompom on the top of my hat cover. I thought the colors looked better on me than they did on Jamie, but I doubted a female within a hundred miles would agree with me.

For the first time, I'd be breaking with a full field of twelve. Behind us were eight exercise riders they'd hired from the track's backstretch. They rode our barn's horses, and wardrobe had decked them out in colorful silks. I'd bet money that Zalaya had two columns for expenses in the wardrobe file.

Gabriel and his assistant followed our entourage in the camera truck. The two of us had shared a short but interesting conversation the previous night in the hotel lobby. When I'd explained what I'd seen in the file. His lips had thinned into an angry line. Today, we were avoiding eye contact afraid our faces would show too much.

Will, who'd been at the barn earlier, had watched me like a hawk but never said a word. I hated the way that made me feel.

Leaning forward, I patted London Fog's dappled neck and felt myself relax. Greta and Jerry had been exercising the two "champions" on the days Jamie and I had been stuck in the sound stage. They'd been doing a good job, because both horses were on their toes. London Fog's muscles had tightened. up and he looked more like the good race horse he'd been bred to be.

I wondered if the horse's previous owner and trainer had given up on him too soon. I'd seen it happen before, especially with trainers who used a one-size-fits-all approach. Today, London felt and looked like the horse he'd been—a horse that could win a stakes race. Despite the fact it was all pretend, my blood ticked up.

In today's race scene, Dillon and Fay were riding a prep race for the big stakes. Dillon was supposed to win this round, but I wondered about the next race. I'd finally managed to weasel a bit of information from Gabriel.

Almost whispering, he'd said the script writers had chosen the Santa Anita Handicap, a Grade I race for horses four-years-old and up. It was run annually in early March and considered one of the most important races for older horses in North America. The kind of race I'd never been lucky enough to ride in.

After he'd told me the name, Gabriel said, "You repeat this to anyone, I'll say you're a liar." Running anxious fingers through his hair he'd said, "*Mon Dieu*, I shouldn't have told you."

"Gabriel," I'd said, "chill. My lips are zipped."

Apparently, his excitement over filming the race had outweighed his caution.

"We're hiring hundreds of extras to fill the stands. They'll shout and scream as you and Dillon come down the stretch. The winner's circle will swarm with cable news and network crews! It will be a scene most fabulous!"

Remembering the passion in his voice, I smiled. Leaning forward, I whispered to London Fog. "You ready to win the Santa Anita Handicap, big boy?"

Though it was all pretend, my words injected a thrill of excitement in my veins. London felt it through the reins and humped his back, readying for a buck.

"Hey, none of that!" I said, grabbing a handful of mane as my legs tightened their grip.

Riding next to me, Jamie grinned. "Don't worry, London. She has the same effect on me."

Behind us, Greta snickered.

Moments later, we were in the metal stalls, each horse's head held by a member of the gate crew. The temporary tracks were laid on the dirt again, and the rolling cart's camera had already filmed us going in. Now it rolled ahead to film us as we busted out.

I settled deeper into the saddle and crossed the rubberized reins over London's dark mane. I grasped the cross with my left hand and grabbed mane with my right. Flopping back in the saddle when the horses rocketed out the gate is something I learned to avoid early on. Having it happen on film would be beyond embarrassing.

There was a moment of dead quiet. Then the track announcer cried, "They're all in line."

Outside our cage door the dirt track stretched into the distance. Suddenly, the bell shrilled, the doors crashed open, and we were off! With the moving rainbow of colored silks, and riders screaming encouragement, it was hard to believe I wasn't riding a real race.

As two of the extras rushed to the lead, London and I were bumped sharply by one of our stable's horses. I yelled at his rider, while steadying London to help him regain his stride. He did, and we flew into and around the first turn.

The original two leaders clung to their positions in front. After our bumpy start, we were left with a wall of horses churning before us. Though everyone knew I had to finish second, this was too much like a real race. The riders were hot and filled with intent.

A hole opened up in front of me, and I asked London to go through. He did not disappoint. He was bold and had ability, a nice combination in a racehorse. He had speed too. In no time, I was almost up with Jamie again, behind the two leaders.

I hoped London had the stamina to go the distance. It would be embarrassing if the other riders had to pull their horses because London faltered in the final furlongs. There were five horses ahead of me as we went into the far turn. I managed to ease London past two of them, leaving only Jamie and the two leaders.

The two horses ahead of Jamie and me were either starting to fade, or their riders were slowing them. Either way things were working out nicely. As we tore down the home stretch, Jamie and I were on the lead. I was sitting on a ton of horse and hoped I'd have the ability to let Jamie win without it being obvious.

I needn't have worried. As I came abreast of Jamie, Mystery Ride dug in and inched ahead of us. To make sure Jamie got the win, I stopped asking London, and he stopped giving. Mystery Ride won by a head. From the camera truck, Gabriel gave us a delighted grin and a thumbs up.

As we galloped out, Jamie said, "Good job, Nikki! So, how do you feel about me whipping and driving us into a dead heat tonight?"

"You," I said, "are incorrigible." But I could feel a smile lurking in the corners of my mouth, and a flush of heat in my cheeks. Looking to change the subject, I said, "If this had been a real race, I'd be thrilled, 'cause this was just the tightener London needs to win the big race."

Jamie gave me a Dillon smirk, "We'll see what the script says about that."

When we reached the barn, Orlando took London and began walking him around the shedrow to cool him out. Anxious to see how quickly London recovered from the race, I walked alongside Orlando. The gleam of his double gold earrings reflected the late morning light.

The dirt beneath our feet had recently been hosed to keep it moist and free of dust. The scent of sweet feed mixed with the smell of damp earth and horse sweat made me feel right at home.

"Nikki, I watch the race," Orlando said. "You still got it! You should be jockey again."

When I shrugged, he said, "What? You want to be movie *chica* now?"

"I'm not sure what I want." The truth of that statement hit me hard. I was twenty-seven years old, having an affair with a twenty-three-year-old movie star. I'd lost Will's respect and friendship, and I had no idea what I'd be doing in the future to earn a living.

Orlando glanced at my face and frowned. "Hey, I *know* you, Nikki. You figure it out. You always do, no?"

I answered with a spread of my palms and a shake of my head. After that, we walked the horse in silence until I could see London was cooling out quickly and seemed none the worse for the wear. As I left them, I glanced at Orlando. "Let me know if he cleans up his feed this evening."

"*Por supuesto.*"

I stood still a moment, watching Orlando and London's impressive set of dappled hindquarters move away down the shedrow. Maybe I could ride again, rebuild my racing career. While filming *The Final Furlong,* I'd felt the familiar emotions of tension, excitement, and joy. What I hadn't felt was the sheer terror I'd experienced after the pain of my bad fall and the long hospital stay.

When I turned back to check that London's stall was ready for his return, I found Greta sitting on a hay bale next to the barn wall. She was drinking a beer and had an opened six pack at her feet. A shaft of bright sunlight had found its way under the shedrow roof and illuminated her blond braids as well as the sweat and dust they'd collected during the long hours spent at the track that day.

She held up another beer can that glistened with droplets of condensation. "Join me for a cold one?"

"Don't mind if I do." I flopped next to her on the hay bale and took a long, frosty sip. "Hits the spot," I said, feeling my lips curving in a satisfied smile.

At the sound of footsteps, I turned my head to see Will approaching. Tension flowed into me, as cold as the beer.

Looking only at Greta, he smiled. "Good job today, Greta. Especially since I know the long hours you keep. Estrella's lucky to have you."

She thanked him for the compliment, then watched him with an odd expression as he walked away without a word to me.

"I thought you two were friends, Nikki. What happened?"

Telling the truth was a nonstarter, so I said, "Jamie happened."

I didn't like saying it, because Will was bigger than that. It was not Jamie that had torn us apart, it was Will's realization that I was lying to him.

Greta grinned. "So, you're saying Will's been scorched by the breath of the green dragon?"

"Yeah," I lied, "he's jealous." I drained my can and rose from the hay bale. "Thanks for the beer. I should probably get going."

"The call of the movie camera," she said. "And Jamie Jackson. I wouldn't mind being in your shoes."

*Yeah, you would.* She had no idea, and I had to keep it that way. I left thinking I'd like nothing better than another beer and to spill everything to Greta. Keeping secrets tore me up. I hated it.

I dug a hand into my jeans pocket and touched the cold metal of the duplicate key to Zalaya's office. I had to see what was in that other file, open it, and let all the secrets loose.

# 25

The next day Reddinger, Millie, Jamie, and I, along with assorted extras, spent long hours filming in the sound stage. There was no chance to sneak into Zalaya's office with so many people around. The camera and sound crew worked hard, shooting scene after scene, Zalaya pushing hard as if he was desperate to finish his film.

He was like a cat with a firecracker tied to its tail. His eyes constantly darted as if looking for a way out. Had someone caught the scent of stolen money and started tracking Zalaya's trail of embezzlement? If so, he should be scared.

I'd started with wardrobe and makeup at 7:00 a.m., before filming a scene where Fay goes to Reddinger for advice on how to best ride her champion in the upcoming Santa Anita Handicap. If Gabriel hadn't already told me, the day's script would have been the first I'd known about the handicap.

It was also the first scene I'd done alone with Reddinger and as I'd always been a big fan of him and his western series, I felt a little giddy. As I said my lines, I did my best to show my fear about such an important race and riding against a top jockey like Dillon.

Except, Zalaya made me do it again, and this time I made it believable. Reddinger was such a good actor, he pulled me right into the scene. He put a fatherly hand on my shoulder, his piercing blue eyes studying my face with affection as he spoke his lines.

"Look, Fay, you know damn well this is going to be a two-horse race. The horses you and Dillon are riding outclass anything in the field. It's your race to lose."

With a gentle finger, he tilted my chin up. "Dillon's a rogue, kid. He'll do whatever he can get away with to win. But he doesn't think of his horse the way you do. You just ride your race and try to stay out of his way. You've got a damn good shot to win this thing."

Reddinger's sympathetic act was so good, I felt like throwing my arms around him and sobbing my thanks. But that wasn't in the script, so I nodded and said, "I'll do my best."

"I don't doubt it, kid. And remember, it's a horse race. Anything can happen."

Zalaya shouted, "Cut," and I was told to get to wardrobe and change for the next scene. Another one of those Dillon and Fay bedroom scenes. Thank God there were only three in the movie. At least I hoped this was the last one.

When I arrived at the trailer, Pinky reached into hanging rows of designer clothes and handed me a set of short cotton voile pajamas. The top and bottom were gauzy and white.

"Strip before you put these on," she said before glancing at my face. Whatever my face told her, made her smile.

"Don't worry, I've got a robe for you to wear until the scene starts.

But what about after the scene started? Things I didn't want showing were embarrassingly visible beneath such flimsy fabric! I intended to use Dillon's sheet and covers to every possible advantage, and if Zalaya didn't like it, he could take a hike.

The makeup girl sat me on her stool, used a lip plumping dark pink gloss and painted my eyes until they were smoky and alluring. Oh yeah, I was going to hang on to those bed covers, all right.

"You've got about twenty minutes," Pinky said. "Zalaya wants you to read these now."

She handed me my sides and I was relieved to see that Dillon had lots of lines, and I only had a few. My raw edge of nerves softened a little as I realized my flimsy top had no buttons, zippers, or ties. Additionally, no one had showed up with a glass of bourbon. Quickly, I read the script. This was not a sex scene, but a scene where Dillon would show he was starting to really care about Fay.

*Who would believe that?*

About the time I was securely belting my robe, Pinky's radio clicked on. A male voice said, "We need Fay in five."

"She's ready," Pinky responded. She grinned at me when the radio went off. "Give 'em hell, kid!"

I was lying in Dillon's bed pretending to be asleep. Who sleeps with a stage light in their face? Even more ridiculous, who sleeps wearing perfect makeup? This had always bugged me about movies and TV, but I guess it's all about the fantasy.

Dillon was awake, already dressed, sitting quietly at his desk reading a track condition book.

The silence was broken by Zalaya's voice. "Listen up, everyone, Fay is waking up. And action!"

I stretched, yawned, and sat up, one hand holding the sheet over my breasts.

"Cut! No, no, no," Zalaya said. "Fay has a lovely figure. Don't hide it."

After glaring at him, I settled back into the bed, once again shutting my eyes.

"Action!"

Again, I yawned, and sat up, letting the sheet fall to my waist. I told myself to get a grip. Everyone in this room had seen or filmed thousands of naked breasts and mine were covered. Well, mostly.

Dillon rose from his chair, and sat on the edge of the bed, focusing on my face. He began his lines and his voice was so real. It was the voice of a man who was in unknown territory, a voice that was no longer cocky or so confident.

He told Fay he was falling in love with her, stopped and shook his head, before continuing.

"I don't know what's wrong with me but as much as I don't want you to win, I'll be happy for you if you do."

"I can't believe you're saying this," Fay said, her fingers clasping Dillon's hand.

He laughed. "I can't either. But I mean it. Let's be careful when we ride tomorrow, okay? If anything happened to you out there, I–I couldn't stand it."

His expression, his tone, was just sweet enough to break a girl's heart. But he still gave the impression of a young man who was all male.

The scene called for Fay to sit up higher, lean into Dillon as he put his arms around her before he gently pressed her back into the pillows. He kissed me then, and it was so sweet that I moaned, just like Fay was supposed to do.

For a wild moment I considered what it would be like if this man really loved me. The thought left me trembling. I was so lost in the scene I forgot Gabriel was barely inches away with his Cannon.

I was jolted back to reality when Zalaya, yelled, "Cut! Good job, you two."

"Yes," Gabriel said. "I see champagne in your immediate future."

It hit me then, that I was done for the day, and except for the upcoming race, I might be done with the movie. But they would be shooting more scenes inside the pretend grandstand and I could come back the next day to watch, and hopefully get into that file cabinet. Unless I could get Gabriel to bring me back tonight.

I stood, quickly shrugging into my robe before belting it tightly. Dillon who had behaved so much like Jamie was watching me. "You have to let me take you to dinner tonight, Nikki. No arguments, we deserve a night out."

Gabriel, who was walking away, turned back. "I'm off to grab that bottle of champagne so you two can start your evening now."

I gave Gabriel a lift of my brows trying to signal my question about getting into the file later. He ignored me. With one more try, I said, "Jamie, it's been a long day and—"

"Nikki, I really want to see you tonight, and I need to talk to you about something. Please?"

"Okay," I said, fighting a thrill of excitement. Did I think he was going repeat the sweet words Dillon had just said to Fay? Why would I let such a crazy thought loose in my head? Somebody should slap me.

# 26

Jamie loved to be in the spotlight. Maybe he *needed* the attention, the reassurance that he was a star. Instead of meeting outside our rooms and going to the hotel garage together, he asked me to wait for him on the sidewalk of the Marriott's circular driveway.

For the occasion, I'd worn a short, red dress borrowed from wardrobe and had carefully applied my makeup. I'd copied the dark and smoky style the makeup artist had done earlier. To top it off, I'd slipped into high heels. This new attention to style and glamor was so unlike me. But hey, I was in a movie, only forty minutes outside of L.A. So, when in Hollywood, why not do as the stars do?

Nearby, a middle-aged couple in comfortable tourist attire were snapping pictures of me with their cellphones. Apparently, I'd achieved "the look." The sudden low rumble of the Carrera's powerful engine, the gleam of its metallic blue paint, and the ridiculously attractive movie star driving it had the tourists' fingers furiously pressing camera buttons.

I climbed into the car and as we drove away, the way the woman's camera was panning us told me she was in video mode. Making her own Hollywood movie.

I almost laughed out loud. Being with Jamie always lifted my spirits, temporarily quelling my fear and doubts. Leaning my head against the headrest, I drank in the cool California air, savoring the mingled scents of eucalyptus trees, blooming flowers, and the rich leather smell of the car's leather upholstery.

When I glanced at Jamie's face, he was watching until his gaze shifted back to the road. Maybe three heartbeats later he slipped a hand onto my thigh.

"You look hot in red, babe."

I sighed. I felt luxurious and sexy. At this moment, there was no place I'd rather be and no one I'd rather be with.

At the Derby restaurant, we sat at the same corner table by the rose-colored brick walls and the framed print of California Chrome. As my fingers traced the smooth starched tablecloth, the waiter delivered our bourbons.

Placing my hand on Jamie's, I said, "So what did you want to talk to me about?"

He picked up his drink. "I want to make a toast."

He nodded at my drink, so I picked it up. Instead of starting his toast, he took a long sip of bourbon. "This is good stuff, Nikki. Have a slug."

"I thought you were making a toast." What was he up to? Still no point in wasting good liquor, so I swallowed some.

"To us," he said lifting his glass. "We've made a damn good team, and I'm—I'm going to miss you when I'm gone."

I stared at him. He wouldn't meet my gaze. His eyes drifted to a spot over my shoulder. "I have a new contract. It's quite brilliant, actually—a movie in Australia with some really big names."

Right, I thought. Big names. Unlike Millie who, after all, was only a soap star, and Reddinger, a mere television actor. And then there was me, a total nobody.

I almost gasped for air as waves of unwanted emotions crashed through me. Pain, anger, humiliation. Mostly, I felt like a fool. Stalling for time, I took another sip of my drink, mentally cringing when I remembered Will's comment about me becoming a shooting star.

I looked at Jamie's face. He was so young. I suddenly felt old, as outdated as yesterday's news. I downed another slug of liquor. It didn't help. Anger blossomed until it overwhelmed my other emotions.

I slammed my glass onto the table. "So, you're moving up in the world? You've conquered England and America. And now you take on Australia."

I hated the bitterness in my voice. At least I stopped myself from saying he should have no trouble finding a new playmate. Liquor had splashed from my glass onto the tablecloth. Not caring, I drank more and tried to stop sounding like a jealous harpy.

"I'm happy for you Dillon. You're a great actor and you have a terrific future ahead of you." I was such a liar.

"You just called me Dillon," he said.

"Isn't that who you are? I mean you're also Jamie, but Dillon is never far behind, is he?"

"I thought you'd take this better, Nikki. It's not like you're a child, is it? You're twenty-seven years old, right? I have my life, and you have yours. Knowing you has been wonderful and sweet. But you knew it had to end, yeah?"

I was saved from answering by our waiter who came to take our order. I looked at Jamie and shook my head.

Jamie smiled at the waiter. "We just came in for the drink."

As the waiter left to get our bill, I drained my glass. Thank God Jamie didn't know about my absurd fantasy of us being together. I had to get a grip. The more upset I acted, the more obvious it would be that I might have harbored such stupid thoughts.

"So, when do you leave?" I asked.

"Almost all of my scenes are wrapped up except for the race. They'll be filming it in the next few days, and then I'm on a plane."

"I hope this goes well for you, Jamie." Good for me, I sounded almost normal.

"You know, I really do adore you, Nikki. There's no point in parting too soon, is there? How about we go back to the hotel, order some steaks and drinks up to my room and talk this out?"

And have sex? "No, I don't think so, Jamie. I want to go to *my* room and get some rest, okay?"

He frowned. "Yeah, sure. Whatever you want."

I felt the sting of tears behind my eyelids. The last time he'd said, "Whatever you want," the words had been like the caress of a lover. Now they sounded more like an annoyed teenager with a classic "*whatever.*"

The fantasy was over. Stick a fork in me, I was done.

I held it together until Jamie dropped me off outside the hotel. I made it to an empty elevator, and the doors slid shut. Then I burst into tears, feeling even more stupid for crying. How had I allowed myself to fall so hard for this guy? Just because he was beautiful, smart, funny, and a fabulous lover?

The elevator doors opened at my floor and fortunately, there was no one around. I flew down the hall to my room where I threw myself on the bed and let the tears rip. Privacy is a good thing, especially when mascara and eyeliner are running down your face.

When the torrent ended, I got up and washed my face. I needed to talk to someone, but Carla, the mentor I'd loved, was dead, and my lifestyle of moving track to track and town to town didn't lend itself to finding and keeping a best friend. I liked Greta and would have called her, but it was almost nine and she had to get up at four every morning.

Will had been closer to a best friend than anyone else, and he wouldn't even speak to me.

Damn it, Nikki. Stop the pity party, get into that other file, and do what you can to protect yourself. I needed to talk to Will in private, tell him what was going on. Screw the thugs. Will knew how to take care of himself, and he had access to the FBI.

Decision made; I was suddenly starving. I ordered up a burger and fries, devoured them when they came, and crawled into bed. I didn't expect to sleep, but at least I could rest my body while my brain whirled around the obstacles that faced me.

# 27

Considering how upset I'd been the previous night, I was surprised when the morning light roused me from a deep sleep. Equally surprising was a new certainty that what I mourned for wasn't real. It was a Jamie Jackson fantasy. The affair was like a scene from a movie. I could almost hear Gabriel yelling, "Cut, it's a wrap."

I'd been afraid that I'd never get over Jamie. Now, I knew I could and would. And I'd surely be glad when the damn movie was over. I wanted to get back to my normal life. In movieland, what was real and what wasn't shifted like quicksand. I wanted to walk on solid ground before I got sucked under.

Time to look ahead. Except for the race, which would be the last scene in *The Final Furlong,* I wasn't scheduled to act again. I knew that Millie and Reddinger, along with some of the supporting actors, would be working the sound stage today.

I planned to watch the day's filming, but first, I needed the grounding sensation that getting on a horse always provided. A ride with Greta and Jerry would ease some of my tension. I dressed in riding clothes, stopped for breakfast at the coffee shop, and drove to the track.

At the barn, Orlando greeted me with a smile, his teeth gleaming white against his olive skin. His double gold earrings flashed in the morning sun.

"Nikki, I knew you would decide horses are better than the camera, yes?"

"Horses are better than anything," I said.

Greta appeared from Mystery Ride's stall and walked toward us as Orlando gave me a sly look.

"Even better than movie star?" he asked.

"Especially better than that."

"Trouble in paradise?" Greta asked.

I nodded. "Pretty much."

"So, what happen?" Orlando asked.

"My scene with Jamie Jackson has ended. Anyway, I don't want to talk about him. I want to ride."

Greta nodded. "Best therapy there is."

After checking Stan's chart, I climbed onto London Fog, Greta was aboard Mystery Ride and Jerry showed up in time to ride Predator. We hit the track and slow galloped a mile. The rhythm of London Fog beneath me, the drum of hoofbeats, and the matching cadence of the massive amounts of air pumping in and out of the horses were soothingly familiar. I felt like a baby rocked in her cradle.

After pulling the horses up, Greta and I walked side by side as we rode in, while Jerry fell a few paces behind.

"So, what happened?" Greta asked.

I shrugged. "The movie's about to end. Jamie's going to Australia to start another film, and it's time for me to come down from the clouds."

"Yeah, that was some pretty rare air you were breathing up there."

Suddenly, I giggled. "It sure was! But you know what? I'm glad it's over. I could fall really hard for that guy, and that would have caused some permanent pain."

What I said was true. I hadn't been with him long enough to get my heart broken. Besides, there were much bigger problems to deal with, and Jamie had been a drug that kept me from focusing.

When I turned London Fog over to Orlando, he immediately felt the knee that had been injured with bone chips.

"Any heat?" I asked. I knew the groom checked the horse's knee every day, but we were so close to the "big" race I had to ask.

Frowning, Orlando said, "Nikki, you don't have to ask me that. You know I tell you if anything is wrong!"

"I do, Orlando. That's why I made sure Will hired you."

Orlando's smile flashed white. "Too bad he not hire *el director de fotografía*."

"Gabriel's learning," I said, and headed for the stable washroom to rinse the backstretch dust off my face. I was glad to see the Nikki I knew in the mirror. No makeup, standard black turtleneck, jeans, and boots.

I gave myself a little salute in the mirror and headed for my car and the sound stage. For all my bravado about getting over Jamie, I hoped he wouldn't be there. It would be fine with me if I didn't see him until the race. I was also glad I hadn't run into Will that morning.

On the way to the sound stage, I stopped at an electronics shop and found a more expensive burner phone that also took pictures. A short time later, I drove through Estrella's security gate and after handing over my thug cellphone, I parked in the lot near the open bay door. I walked past the huge RV and headed for the long side-hall to peek through the two-way mirrors. I wanted to know who was present and where they were before I approached the film set.

Of course, the real reason I'd come was to find a way into that file in Zalaya's office without getting caught. If I could get into his computer, I might really hit paydirt. All the more reason to know who was there and where.

I double-timed it past the window that gave a view into Dillon's apartment set. I didn't want to stir those memories. No one was in there. Millie's set was empty as well. I kept going and passed by the Chandelier room, once again marveling how the wall cut in like a long slanting dormer window to allow for the set of stairs on the other side. I found the cast and crew in the Player's Club.

Millie was sitting on one of the leather couches with Dillon. They appeared to be in earnest conversation. Reddinger was off-camera waiting on the side. I recognized some of the extras who were at the betting windows or playing the role of pari-mutuel clerks taking in the money while their machines spit out tickets.

Zalaya was watching Millie and Dillon as Gabriel and his assistant filmed. I kept going until I hit the end wall with the green screen that brought the race-track to life. Currently, that screen was off.

Reversing, I trotted down the hall looking through every window. No one had changed their location, nor had anyone else arrived. I took a deep breath and sped through the hall to Zalaya's office. I pulled the key from my jeans pocket and stopped outside the office door.

Standing still, I listened for a voice or the sound of footsteps heading my way. I only heard the soft whistle of air from the HVAC system and a faint rumble and clacking from clothing Pinky must have put in the trailer's dryer. Pressing my ear to the wooden door, I listened some more. Nothing. I slid the key in the lock and went inside, closing the door behind me.

I left it unlocked. If Zalaya showed up, I could say the door had been open. *Yeah, like that would keep me out of trouble.*

Digging into my other pocket, I pulled out the metal picks I'd swiped from Larry the Locksmith and went to work on the second file drawer.

Inside, each file was labeled Estrella Studio, with a string of six numbers and letters after the word Studio. Had to be some sort of code because the characters on each of the dozen or so files made no sense. At least not to me. Was this just more of Zalaya's money fleecing?

With an ear towards the door, I quietly pulled out the first file and opened it. The paper inside named a company called Film Enterprises. There was a lot of legal jargon about their investment in the movie *Final Furlong*. If I was reading it correctly it looked like this company based in Bolivia had invested almost five million in the film.

The next file named another company. Artistic Productions was located in Venezuela and had supposedly sunk ten million into the film. That was weird since Venezuela was a bankrupt, socialist country. Who would want to do business with them? Quickly scanning through the file, I discovered that Artistic Productions was owned by yet another company based in Panama. This one was called South Atlantic Enterprises.

These must be the various investors in *The Final Furlong*. And if so, would I find Vos's name in one of the files? No way I had time to search them all. Using the new phone's camera, I snapped photos of the names and companies in the first six files. By that time, I was too nervous to continue. I'd already pushed my luck just being in Zalaya's office for almost twenty minutes, twenty of the most nerve-wracking minutes I'd ever spent. I closed the file drawer, locked it, and scooted from the office, breathing a sigh of relief when I was in the hall and no one was around.

When I could, I'd ask Gabriel if I could talk to him later. Maybe the photos I'd taken would mean more to him. If I could talk him into it, I'd have him stand lookout again while I tried to access Zalaya's computer. I bet I could find his password taped under a drawer or hidden in a similar location.

Right now, it seemed wise to show up on set as if I had just arrived to watch some of the day's filming. As I hurried past the huge RV, the sound of the tumbling dryer became louder. Nearby, the scent of laundry detergent rode the air that spilled through the exhaust fan. Moving swiftly through the sound stage, I passed the two apartment sets, the Chandelier Room, and reached the Player's Club.

The crew was filming Reddinger, Millie, and one of the supporting actors. They were discussing the upcoming race. The supporting actor played an over-confident braggart, touting his horse that would be running against Millie's. She glanced at Reddinger and rolled her eyes.

Jamie was off set, on the side, and when he saw me, his lips tightened and he looked away. Was he mad that I'd turned him down the previous night? For God's sake he was the one who'd announced his sudden departure. How I would have loved to march over and say, "Gee, Jamie, I thought you would have taken me turning you down better. After all, you're twenty-three."

Of course, I didn't. Instead, I just pretended to focus on the scene unfolding before us. My previous feelings of humiliation and loss had broken loose and were galloping unbridled through my head.

*Deep breath, Nikki. Let it out slow. Repeat.*

I got my emotions under control as the scene finished. Zalaya told everyone to break for lunch and we went to an area on the far side of the RV. Estrella's catering company had set up tables and chairs and were serving sandwiches, so-das, and Pellegrino sparkling water.

When I sat at a table next to Gabriel, Jamie chose a different one and sat with his back to me. He was pouting like a child. I realized he was delightful to be around as long as he got his own way. So, what had I lost? Not a damn thing.

"What are you grinning about," Gabriel asked me.

"Oh, just stuff."

"Ah, the all-inclusive 'stuff.' What would Americans do without that word?"

"Be forced to tell the truth?"

Gabriel raised his hands in mock horror. "*Quelle horreur!* Not the truth!

We exchanged grins. I had grown quite fond of the Frenchman, and we sat in companionable silence while we ate. His fear of being seen talking to me seemed to have lessened. After all we did have to work together. Surely those two lowlifes, Gold Necklace and Diamond Ring understood that much.

But while Gabriel and I relaxed and enjoyed our lunch, Zalaya, picked at his food. Once, his eyes darted about as if he were afraid. He sipped his water and suddenly pushed his plate away, stood, and hurried toward his office.

I was pretty sure I'd left everything in his office exactly as I'd found it. But suppose I hadn't? The thought sent a frisson of fear through me, but there was nothing I could do about it now.

# 28

After a silent prayer I'd left no sign of my intrusion in Zalaya's office, I glanced at my watch. The actors had a half-hour of break time left, and I wanted to use to opportunity to talk to Gabriel in private.

"Will you come with me," I asked, "while I step outside for some air?"

"There is no time for that. The next scene, it commences soon.

*"Please?"* I said giving what I hooped was a beseeching look.

He muttered something in French. I'd learned this was his standard response to being irritated but also resigned. I pushed my chair back, stood, and gestured toward the bay door.

"Come on. A few minutes of fresh air and sunshine will do you good." Rising from his chair, he followed me outside the building.

I led him around a corner of the rectangular building, to one of the end walls. Craning my neck, I scanned the wall and roofline for cameras. There was one above us, but it was directed toward the hedges and fence, more evidence of Estrella's determination to stop the press or anyone else from accessing the studio.

"Gabriel, look at this," I said pulling the new burner from my tote bag.

He stepped back quickly like the phone might bite him.

"No, listen. I got into that other file, and I'm confused about what I saw. What is this?"

He glanced at the first photo. It was the file page that listed Artistic Productions as a Venezuelan outfit that had supposedly sunk ten million into the film. The next photo revealed the identity of the true owner, a totally different company based in Panama.

Using his fingers, he made the photos bigger. He stared for a few seconds before a gasp escaped him. Then he scrolled through all the photos, before shutting the phone down and shoving it back at me.

"*Merde!* You need to erase these! If anyone sees them your life could end!"

"Why? What is this stuff?"

Gabriel's eyes were wide with fright. "These things make sense now. Why didn't I see it before?"

"See *what?*"

"Money laundering. These are shell companies! Estrella is money laundering and Zalaya must be managing it for them through the film. This is a big operation, far worse than Zalaya's skimming. He is a fool to cheat these people!"

"What people?" I was so frustrated with half-answers, I almost shouted the question.

"Arjun, those thugs with the jewelry. Vos. I didn't *want* to know. I just want to make my movie then get away as fast as possible."

I grabbed his arm. "Away from what? Tell me, Gabriel!"

"The *cartel!* The Martinez drug cartel. Arjun's a Martinez. I told myself maybe he was just a distant relative. Now I fear it is much worse. I think his brother, Lexo Martinez runs the cartel in Panama. They are bloodthirsty. They kill for fun."

The air and sun faded away as my brain raced forward like a loose horse plunging over a cliff.

"They killed him," I whispered. "They killed Dave."

Gabriel nodded, his face was miserable and tight, mirroring my own anxiety.

"Gabriel, we've got to be strong. You have to go inside for the next scene. I–I'll follow you in and watch as if I'm interested and happy to be there."

He took a long breath. "Can you do that?"

"I have to. Besides, we are only conjecturing. We don't *know* anything, right?"

"*Oui. Je ne sais rien.*" He repeated the words several times, like a mantra. I assumed he was telling himself he knew nothing, steeling himself to go inside and act normal.

He exhaled a long breath and disappeared through the bay door. I followed at a distance, thinking I would walk the hall of mirrors once more to see if I picked up a negative vibe emanating from Zalaya or his office. It would be easier to put my "happy mask" in place if I knew I hadn't been discovered.

I entered the hall and glanced at the closed office door. Walking softly, I reached it and listened. Hearing nothing, I breathed a sigh of relief and turned to look through the mirrors to see if things appeared normal.

As I worked my way toward the Player's Club, each set I passed was empty. A glance at my watch told me they'd be live on set in about five minutes. Everything seemed fine. So why did I suddenly feel such a strong sense of foreboding?

As I glanced through the window into the Player's Club, I noticed everyone was in place except Zalaya. He wasn't there. I was trying to figure what this meant when I heard shouting behind the rear exit door. Afraid, I darted back to the deep dormer-like bay that was the backside of the staircase in the Chandelier Room. As it descended to ground level, the bay's height shrank to about two feet.

I heard the exit door crash open and risked a peek around the corner. Zalaya, looking wild with fear stumbled in my direction. His face had been beaten and one eye was so swollen and bloody, I doubted he could see much as tried to run ran past me. He had hurt his leg somehow and was moving slowly.

Diamond and Gold, burst through the exit door. Now that I knew they were Martinez thugs, I cringed. *Shit*.

I double-timed it deeper into the staircase bay, dropped to my knees and scooted as far as I could into the low end. There was no light back here, and I prayed I was hidden. Zalaya was almost past me when they caught him.

"Please!" he gasped.

"You're a fool, Zalaya. You thought we wouldn't know you're stealing from Martinez?"

"No! Please. I haven't. I didn't. I-I'm sorry," Zalaya begged.

As a thick wire appeared in Diamond's hand, Gold clapped his palm over Zalaya's mouth to keep the struggling director quiet.

Diamond looped the wire around Zalaya's neck, pulled it tight, and I watched in horror as Zalaya struggled for air he could no longer breathe. His eyes bugged out and a sudden release of urine darkened his pants.

I stifled a scream. A wave of nausea hit me. If I retched, I'd be found. Unable to watch his final struggles, I closed my eyes. But I could hear him. It was sickening. A moment later everything stopped, leaving a dead silence that told me Zalaya was gone.

When I opened my eyes, I'd swear Diamond was staring straight at me. My hands grew cold and shook with fear. These men would kill me. But if Diamond could see me, he didn't show it. Instead, the two of them used their shoulders to prop up Zalaya and began dragging him toward the exit.

I told myself to breathe, to wait, and to listen. When I heard the exit door open and close, I crawled forward. Staying on my hands and knees until I reached the hall, I peered around the corner. Empty. Lurching to my feet I raced to Zalaya's office, burst through the unlocked door, and bolted it.

I grabbed the burner. I *should* call 911. Instead, I called Will Marshall.

"What do you want Nikki?"

Even now, the chill in his voice hurt.

"Will I'm so sorry. I should have told you everything, but they threatened to *kill* you. They murdered Zalaya. They're dragging him away now. It's *horrible.* I'm so scared. You've got to help me, Will, please!"

"Nikki, you're not making any sense. For Christ's sake, get a grip and tell me. *Slowly.* First, tell me where you are, then start at the beginning."

I was so relieved to hear his voice, I burst into tears.

"Come on, Nikki. Take a breath. *Talk* to me."

I wiped my tears with the back of my wrist and told him.

# 29

As I finished telling Will about the files I'd discovered in Zalaya's office, what Gabriel said they meant, and the horror of Zalaya's murder, my voice rattled like dead leaves in a November wind.

"You've locked yourself in Zalaya's office, right?" Will asked.

"Yes."

"Stay there, Nikki. Don't move. Martinez's men will have to get rid of Zalaya's body. They're probably long gone. But don't bet your life on it."

Will sounded like he was moving. I could hear pounding footsteps through the phone, then the sound of a car engine roaring to life.

"On my way," he said. "You stay put!"

"Will, please. Can you stay on the line 'til you get here?" I realized I was begging.

"Sorry, Nik. I have to call the TRPB so they can get this information to the FBI. We think the Feds don't know the extent of this. Since the murder took place in Detective Garcia's jurisdiction, I have to call him, too."

"Can't you have Garcia send a bunch of cops?"

"No. We can't blow the lid off this thing until the FBI's in place. We move too soon, everyone will disappear. People that know too much will be executed. We'll be lucky if we can still catch the assholes that murdered Zalaya. Hold on, I'll be there in five."

He hung up and left me alone with my dread.

*People that know too much will be executed.* I pictured the wire tightening around Zalaya's neck. I yanked the trash can towards me, sure I was going vomit. I forced some slow breaths and fought off the sickness.

Damn you, Will. I could have done without those words. My little flash of anger steadied me, and I realized how relieved I was to have finally told him the

156

truth. I'd hated that he'd been convinced I was a liar. That I would take money to keep quiet. That I was more interested in being a movie star than in doing what was right.

*You should know me better than that, Will.* But then I hadn't trusted him either. It was an ugly wound between us I feared might never heal.

I tried to push these thoughts away. Gabriel must think I'd been too afraid and had bailed on him. He was another one who knew too much and the knowledge made me shudder. I really liked the Frenchman. He needed to be protected. And what was the FBI going to do? Try and set up some sort of sting operation? How long would that take? They'd want me to stay and finish the race scene. But our director was dead so how would that work?

Could they be filming scenes today without Zalaya? I was fairly certain that after a few scenes, only the race remained. But now everything was up in the air. *Stop it Nikki, this isn't your problem. Your problem is staying alive.*

My fear spiraled out of control again. It was cut short by a soft tap on the door. I froze until I heard Will's voice.

"It's me. Open up."

I'd never been so glad to see anybody in my life. Still, I was unable to speak as he stared at me.

"Are you all right?"

I nodded and felt the sting of more tears. Will put his hands on my shoulders, then pulled me in close.

"Nikki Latrelle," he said, "if you'd let anything happen to you, I'd probably kill you myself." He kissed my wet cheek, then held me at arm's length. "Now, stop looking like a deer in Martinez headlights and let's get the hell out of here, okay?"

When I nodded, he grabbed my hand and rushed me through the large bay past the huge RV, and stuffed me into the back seat of his Dodge SUV. The rear windows were heavily tinted.

From behind the wheel, Will shot a look at me. "There's a fly sheet on the floor. Get down there and cover yourself with it. I don't want anyone to know you've left."

That was fine with me. I scrambled to the floor and pulled the fly sheet over me. Seconds later, Will eased the SUV to a stop at the guard house.

He sounded so relaxed as he exchanged pleasantries with the guard. Meanwhile, I was on the floor trying not to scream, "Get me out of here!"

Once he hit the street, the Dodge Durango took off like a starship at warp speed. I grabbed the metal base of the passenger seat in front of me and held on.

"What the hell have you got under the hood of this thing?" I asked from beneath my fly sheet.

"Dodge Viper engine. What, it's too fast for you, Latrelle?"

I was enjoying the distraction. "Seems a shame to hide an engine like that beneath the hood of a Durango. How can this thing handle that engine, anyway?"

"Easy, just a new transmission, specialized suspension, shocks, tires and a built-in roll bar."

"Who paid for that?" I asked.

"What else do I have to spend my money on, Nikki?"

I tried to ignore the emptiness of those last words and how well I understood them. Instead, I forced my attention back to the muscle car.

I'd only seen a real Viper once. I'd been going to Pimlico Racetrack on the Baltimore Beltway and the thing had passed me with a low hum and disappeared before I was sure what had happened. I'd wanted one ever since. As had often been the case in the past, Will and I were drawn to the same things–fast cars, fast horses, and good bourbon.

"The Arcadia PD is just ahead. You can sit up now, Nik."

When I did, we were approaching a large white building, the top of which resembled a flying saucer. Centered at the top was a communications device resembling a long needle with spikes.

We turned into the main entrance. It appeared the entire area around the police department was made of municipal buildings and activities. Signs marked one building as City Hall and a large square of grass as the "Arcadia Soccer Field."

There was also a walled off section of parking with a solid gate and a warning sign that the area was for police vehicles only.

"Can't we go in through the gate to where the cop cars are parked?"

"No, we can't. Garcia is meeting us in the lobby. You can zip inside. I'll worry about parking the car."

"What if Garcia's not there? Do I just stand around the lobby so anyone can see me?" I couldn't control the quiver in my voice.

"Don't worry, he'll be there. He wants to nail these guys as much as we do." He turned around and looked at me.

"Anything else, Latrelle?"

"No." I stayed quiet, though I wanted to talk. Talk about anything that would stop the mental tape of Zalaya's execution playing in my head. The images weren't helping to quell my nausea either.

The SUV reached a sidewalk leading to an entrance. Will's tires squealed to a fast stop in a no-parking area.

"Look," Will said. "I'll dash inside, make sure Garcia is there, okay?" When I nodded, he hurried into the building. A moment later, he jogged back, and after a visual scan of our surroundings, he opened the rear door.

"Come on, Nik. Hurry."

I felt so exposed as I jogged with him to the entrance. Paranoia had me in a cold, tight grip.

Mentally, I sagged with relief when I saw the hard face of Garcia as we darted inside. He motioned me to follow him, as Will left to move the car. Moments later, Garcia and I were behind the closed doors of an elevator and going up. We were met on the second floor by a deep voiced chocolate-skinned cop in a suit. He walked us past a photo memorial to a cop killed in the line of duty.

On either side, the two men escorted me down a wide hall past a wall with the affixed metal letters, "Detectives."

Behind us, the ding of a second elevator and the sound of jogging footsteps announced Will's arrival.

Reaching Garcia's office, we were seated in chairs. They were more comfortable than those of my previous experiences in cop shops. Of course, this time I wasn't a suspect. I was a witness. The fact did little to relieve my anxiety.

Garcia, seated behind his desk, still had those hard cop-eyes and a suit even more rumpled than the one he'd worn when Dave was murdered. That day seemed light years in the past, yet it was only a couple of weeks ago.

The cop who'd met us outside the elevator chose to lean against a wall. His face expressionless, he stared at Will and me. He was younger with softer eyes, but I got a tough as nails vibe from him. He pulled a small notebook and a pen from a pocket as if to take notes.

"You can put that away, Diggs. Mr. Marshall has notified the FBI and agents are on the way from the LA office. No need to go through it all twice."

Diggs frowned, probably not liking the case going to the feds.

Will caught his expression. "Don't worry, Detective Diggs. They'll want your help and from recent experience, I'd say it's more likely they'll work with you rather than over you."

Diggs shot him a I'll-believe-it-when-I-see-it look.

Garcia rose from his desk. "Let's move this to a conference room where we can spread out and be ready to work when these guys arrive."

"Can I use the ladies?" I asked. "And I'd kill for a Diet Coke."

Diggs caught my eye, tilted his head to the door, and I followed him down the hall to a break room with a soda machine. "Ladies is three doors down, on your left."

I thanked him and made a beeline for the bathroom. It was clean and fresh smelling. I used the facilities, washed my hands, and went after the Diet Coke. It could usually sooth an upset stomach. The shot of caffeine wouldn't hurt either.

After a big swallow if ice cold Coke and with can in hand, I saw Diggs up the hall waving me toward a doorway. Seconds later, I entered a fairly large conference room with a long polished-wood table with maybe a dozen chairs around it. Garcia sat at one end, and a man and a woman in neatly pressed, conservative suits sat on the far side of the table. Had to be the feds.

A wave of dizziness hit me, and I realized my hands were shaking again. Will was sitting at the near side of the table. When he saw me, he pulled out a chair next to him, and I sank into it gratefully.

The room smelled of new fabric and paint. The gray carpeting must have been dyed recently. The odor was so strong, it burned in my throat. I took another swallow of Coke. Across from me, a window looked onto the cop parking lot. The wall around it was high enough that the public couldn't see inside, making me feel safer. Then I remembered the sniper on the roof who'd shot Dave.

Not the best memory for the moment. It only reminded me that if a professional is determined to kill you, they probably will. Unless you kill them first.

Diggs placed himself next to Garcia and I could feel the eyes of the feds on me. When I glanced at them, they introduced themselves as Special Agents Halchik and Thompkins. They made a show of producing their FBI ID and flashing it at me, while Diggs rolled his eyes.

Halchik, the woman, had high cheek bones, dark hair, and the ever so slightly slanted eyes of an Eastern European. She should have been a model or an actress. Gabriel and Zalaya would probably love to film her. A shudder ran through me. *What was I thinking?*

I realized everyone had turned to me. Their expressions were expectant. Garcia's brows had risen in question, and one of his hands hovered over a recording machine as if about to turn it on.

"Earth to Nikki," Will whispered in my ear.

"Um, sorry," I said. "It's been a—a rough day. Did you just ask me something?"

Garcia's voice was surprisingly gentle. "Ms. Latrelle, can you tell us what you know about today's events at Santa Anita as they relate to the Estrella film, it's employees and associates?"

I opened my mouth, but nothing came out. Will put his hand on mine. "Give her a minute, people. She just witnessed a brutal murder. I know a lot of what she knows, so how about you let me start, and then Ms. Latrelle can fill in with any specifics known only to her."

"I have no objection," Garcia said. "Are you two okay with that?"

Though the two feds nodded, Agent Thompkins looked at Garcia. "Let's just do this without the recorder until we see what they have to say."

As Will's hand tightened over mine a wave of emotion hit me. I hadn't lost him. My eyes welled with tears. Agent Halchik opened her bag, withdrew a small package of tissues, and slid it across the table.

"Thank you," I said. I was so relieved Will and I were talking. So grateful that we could work *together* again. I'd felt so bereft, as if I'd abandoned myself in a desolate land. It was like a bad dream and now, it had ended.

Will caught my gaze, shook his head, and whispered, "Nikki, what am I going to do with you?"

I gave him a low watt smile. It was all I could muster.

Will reached for the pitcher of water and glasses someone had placed on the table. He poured himself a glass, took a sip, and began to speak.

# 30

An hour later, I was still in the Arcadia PD's conference room, struggling to describe the most horrible part of what I knew.

With my eyes on Garcia, I said, "Like I told you before, I don't know the real names of these guys, so I just call them by the jewelry they wear."

"Straightforward and simple is good," Garcia said, "Just tell us the rest and we can get you two out of here soon."

I drew in some air and took the plunge. "I was hiding in the recess created by the staircase on one of the sets. They caught up with Zalaya right in front of me. It was Diamond that had the wire. Gold restrained the poor guy and Diamond strangled him." My last words came out in a gasp. I was shuddering.

Once again, Will's hand covered mine. "Hey, you're okay, Nik. Just breathe."

I did, and nodding, I said, "I'm all right. It was just so horrible and *disgusting*. Then, they kind of propped him up and dragged him away to the exit door. You people know the rest."

I was waiting for them to say something when I suddenly remembered I had the file photos on the camera in my tote bag. When Halchik leaned across the table toward me, ready to speak, I said, "Wait! You have to see these photos I got from Zalaya's files."

After pulling out the burner I'd bought that morning, I brought the photos up and handed the phone to Halchik. She stared at the pictures then passed the phone to Agent Thompkins before turning back to me.

"Thank you, Ms. Latrelle, you've been a big help. We knew the Martinez cartel was funneling fentanyl and meth amphetamine into the country, but they're a slippery bunch, and we haven't been able to prove our suspicions."

"What are your plans now?" Garcia asked the FBI agents.

Special Agent Thompkins, who didn't look that *special* to me, held up his hand with his palm out when Halchik started speaking. He took over the conversation. As he spoke, he stared at Will and me. Behind his glasses, what I'd previously considered to be mild gray eyes turned to steel.

"We're not here to nail the Martinez cartel for laundering money. That's an offence, of course, but the FBI's interest goes beyond what you know about Estrella and the murder you witnessed today."

"*Two* murders," I said. "We told you, they shot Dave, the assistant cameraman."

"Yes," Thompkins said. "But we can leave that offense in Garcia's hands." He glanced at Garcia, who nodded.

"The big picture is about an organization involved in racketeering and international drug trafficking."

He paused for a sip of water, his face and body language tightening even more. The fierceness in his expression suggested he was more "special" than I'd thought.

"Look, Estrella and the people associated with this movie are in it up to their eyeballs. They've been using the Martinez organization's money to make a movie in a way that can't be traced back to the cartel. So, what you two know about the Estrella film and the people involved is critical to our investigation."

With a knowing smile, Will said, "So, you're going to put the screws to Estrella so they'll cooperate and help you nail the cartel?"

"You're damn right we are!"

Will and Garcia nodded. Me, I was fighting the panic in my gut.

"So," I asked, "what am I supposed to do? To be honest with you, I just want to run!"

"Can't do that, Ms. Latrelle," Thompkins said. "We need your cooperation; we need you on the set acting like it's business as usual."

I closed my eyes. A long sigh and the whispered words, "Oh, God," escaped me.

"We can do this Nikki." Will's voice.

I opened my eyes and looked at the group in the room.

"What about Gabriel Dubois?" I asked. "He's a really nice guy and he's just as scared as I am."

"Don't worry," Thompkins said. "We've already spoken to him."

Startled, I asked, "When did you do that?"

"After Will got you out of the studio. With Zalaya's sudden disappearance Gabriel wrapped up filming for the day. Agents picked him up after he left the soundstage."

"Does he know Zalaya's dead?" I asked.

"He does now."

"He must be *so* scared." I could imagine the Frenchman's fear. It ran neck and neck with mine. How could we possibly be safe?

Will, who knew me so well, turned his gaze from me to Thompkins. "How do you plan to keep Ms. Latrelle safe?"

"And Gabriel," I added.

"You'll both be protected," Thompkins said.

From across the table, Halchik leaned towards me. "I know it's asking a lot, but we really need your help. We can't have people like Vos, and your jewelry-loving thugs realize they've been exposed." She paused to glance at Tompkins, who nodded as if approving her words and indicating she should keep going. Obviously, he had seniority over her.

Halchik's next words were interrupted when Garcia's phone dinged with a text message. After reading it, he used voice-to-text. "Get on that now!"

I could feel tension escalating in the room. Outside the window, I saw two cops running across the pavement of the police car lot. They plunged into a squad car, and with lights flashing and siren screaming, they raced through the exit gate.

Had something happened to Gabriel? I stared at Garcia, wanting to know, but afraid to ask. Thompkins had no such inhibition.

"What is it?" he asked.

"It's a local matter," Garcia responded. "A series of robberies has been plaguing some of Arcadia's mom and pop stores."

A knock on the door seemed to startle everyone. "Got your pizzas," a voice said from the hall.

"Well, bring 'em in." Garcia said. "We need a break." He stood and stretched.

The door opened and the welcome smell of tomato sauce, garlic and cheese wafted pleasantly into the room, canceling the strong odor of fabric dye. I realized I was starving. Diggs left the room to make a fresh pot of coffee, and I followed him out to get another Diet Coke.

When I returned, the atmosphere in the room was downright cheerful. What would we do without our comfort food?

Once Diggs and I settled in with pizza, coffee, and Coke, Halchik continued with what she'd been saying before the squad car had gunned it out of the police lot.

Her eyes settled on me and Will. "Obviously, since the unexplained disappearance of Zalaya, Estrella will be sending someone from LA to help this fellow, Gabriel, finish the film."

I swallowed the bite of pizza I'd been working on. "So, Will and I pretend we know nothing?"

"Can you do that, Ms. Latrelle?" Halchik asked.

I felt a surge of anger at the situation I'd been placed in. "I'll have to if I'm sticking around here. Otherwise, I'll be dead, right?"

"You'll be protected. Both of you," Thompkins said defensively.

"Sure, we will," I said. "Just like Dave and Zalaya."

"Rein it in, Nik. They need you alive to testify," Will said.

I didn't answer him.

Halchik let out a pent-up breath. "Just concentrate on the movie. The Martinez family are businessmen, and they want to make their profit on the film. This necessitates a successful movie, so Estrella will be all over this."

"And you'll be all over them," I said. "They're really going to be between a rock and a hard place."

"That's their problem," Thompkins said. "Not yours."

I didn't answer him. I had a bad feeling about how this would play out, but I kept it to myself.

I was frightened later when I'd been separated from Will. A plain clothes cop, driving a "taxi" returned me to my bugged hotel room. Along with the hidden microphones in my room, my tote bag carried the cartel's iPhone that allowed them to listen to my every word.

Agent Halchik had told me to be careful to use the iPhone as I ordinarily would.

*Yeah, right.*

"Try to act as normal as you can. Use this," she'd said, handing me a fresh burner phone, "for any conversations related to the FBI or Garcia's investigations."

Beside Will, the only person I could talk to was Gabriel and only by burner phone when I was outside the sound stage or my room. Apparently, Gabriel was given the same instructions. I just hoped we could keep our expressions and eyes from communicating our fear and knowledge to the enemy.

I'd never been a real actress, but now I had to be. If I wanted to stay alive.

# 31

At five o'clock that afternoon, fear drove me to pace the length of my hotel suite. At one end, I opened a narrow gap in the closed window drapes and stared at the hotel parking lot before doubling back to gaze through the peep hole in the door to my room.

As I squinted through the security hole, a car alarm went off outside causing me to jump and scurry back to the drapes again. A frazzled looking woman was trying to shut off the annoying honking and flashing headlights with her remote. Finally, she got inside the car and shut the noise off.

I exhaled a breath. The uneasy dread that had followed me to my hotel room reminded me of a very old song from a group called the Buffalo Springfield. When I was little, my mom listened to a lot of that old stuff. At times, I appreciated its simplicity compared to the current electronic music often driven by computerized drums and voiceovers.

Unfortunately, those old notes and lyrics were playing in my head. Something about paranoia striking deep and into my life it would creep. It starts when you're always afraid–

The cartel phone rang, and I yelped like a frightened puppy. Gabriel's name on the screen brought a sense of relief that allowed my hands to unclench. Still, I was nervous about talking to him. Could he play his part? Could I?

I took a breath and opened the call. "Gabriel," I said, "any word from Zalaya?"

"It is quite strange. He has disappeared and no one seems to know where he is."

"So, how do we finish the movie if he doesn't show up?"

"Estrella is playing it safe and sending up a replacement for him tomorrow morning. I don't think they are worried about it, Nikki."

*Wrong. By now they had to know the FBI had them by the short hairs. Who'd want to be squeezed between the FBI and a drug cartel?*

Gabriel was still talking, and reining in my thoughts, I listened.

"Estrella knows that the race and the scene in the winner's circle with Reddinger and Millie are all that remains to be filmed. Oh, and Nikki, you'll be happy to hear this."

Mentally, I cringed, afraid he was about to say something about the cartel. I should have had more faith in him.

"You and London Fog will be the winners!"

"Really? That's great," I said. *Oh boy, Jamie was going to love this.* The thought almost made me giggle. I was pleased enough at this turn of events that my surprise and enthusiasm were real. So far, Gabriel and I were managing to play our roles well.

"Even though they are sending the replacement," Gabriel continued, "Estrella wants to delay the race and final wrap-up for a day."

"So, you're saying we finish the day after tomorrow?"

*"Exactement."*

I could hear the relief in his voice. I felt it too. Two more days and we could get out of this mess, hopefully leave our fear in the dust at the track's finish line. Since it was Tuesday, it meant we'd film the race on Thursday. Friday, Santa Anita would be back to live racing, so we'd better get it right on Thursday, or we'd have to wait almost a week for the next dark day. I said as much to Gabriel.

"I'm not worried," he said. "You, Jamie, and our extra riders work beautifully together. We'll get it done."

"I hope we can film it in one take," I said. "London Fog won a stake at Belmont, but he's not in shape to do multiple takes." And I wasn't sure how long his knee would hold up.

"Don't worry, Nikki. It will all work out."

*Famous last words.*

We ended the call and I dialed room service to order dinner up to my room. Earlier, Will and I had decided it would be safer for both of us to stay in our rooms, order in, and watch a movie. I hoped my cartel spies would enjoy listening to the Jack Reacher movie I planned to watch.

I was reading the room service menu when my phone chirped, startling me yet again. It was Jamie. I almost ignored the call, but curiosity got the better of me.

"Nikki," he said, "I've been acting like an ass."

I didn't disagree, and let the silence grow, waiting to see what else he had to say.

"Look, I can't stop thinking about you. We're really good together."

"And . . ." I stretched the word out.

"I want you to come to Australia with me. Don't worry, I'll pay for everything."

Though jumping on a jet and escaping the cartel with Jamie had some appeal, it wasn't who I was. I almost said, "What? So, I can be your groupie?"

But he had sounded earnest and being snarky would only make our last bit of filming together harder. So, instead, I told him, "Jamie, that's a really nice offer, but I can't. I have obligations. People I don't want to let down."

People like Will, the two FBI agents, Garcia, and Gabriel, who was as scared as I was. I wanted to know that he would be safe when the movie was over. Besides, we'd probably have to testify in court at some point. Disappearing was a coward's way out.

"Jamie, I really like you. And I think you are an amazing actor and have a terrific career ahead of you. I just don't see me being a part of that. It's not what I want to do with my life."

There was a silence while he digested my words. Then he took the high road. "I understand," he said. "But you are an amazing woman and I will miss you."

"And I will be watching every movie you ever make," I said.

"And I hope with a secret smile, yeah?"

I laughed. "Yes, definitely. I'll have a secret smile when I think about those silver buttons."

"Okay then, Nikki. I'll see you at the track."

"Yes," I said, and hung up.

It was a bigger relief than I'd imagined to move that chapter of my life into the past. Not that I'd ever forget him. Who could?

The next morning, room service arrived with coffee, oatmeal and fresh fruit. I donned my exercise jeans and boots and headed to the lobby to find my driver and Town Car waiting beneath the canopy.

Moments later, I passed by the Australian willow and nodded at the security guard. Was he on the Martinez Cartel's payroll or only answerable to Estrella Studio? Was there even a difference anymore?

Stan Gabrino limped from his office onto the shedrow, his eyes washed red with inebriation and lack of sleep. As I walked toward him to say good morning, a strong whiff of booze breath reached my nostrils. No wonder Estrella had hired him. An old timer who wouldn't see beyond his alcoholic fog was just the ticket for Zalaya to do his skimming and for Estrella to keep their mob connection hidden.

Estrella must have hated it when Will showed up. The last thing they needed was the watchful eye of the TRPB endangering their money laundering scheme and connection to the Martinez Cartel.

Nearby, Greta, Jerry, and a bunch of extras stopped their conversation and turned to hear Stan's morning schedule. Most of them carried saddles, feeling safer and more comfortable with their own gear. But Estrella owned the bridles, and the grooms had left them hanging outside each stall, the bits polished, and the leather smooth and clean. I caught Greta's eye and moved next to her, realizing I would miss her.

"Okay, you guys," Stan said, "I want you in a group, jogging the horses you'll be riding in the movie tomorrow. Take 'em a mile round the track, cool 'em out, and put 'em to bed".

No one complained that they were expected to take on the lowly job of hotwalker after they rode. They were too happy with the pay and the chance to be in a movie. I knew Orlando and one of our other grooms would take care of London Fog and Mystery Ride. Being a star had its benefits.

Just then, Jamie came through the gate, his face so beautiful in the morning light that Greta sucked in her breath.

"Damn, he's gorgeous. I hate that I'll never see him again except in the movies."

"You'll get over it," I said.

"Will you?" she asked.

"Yeah, I'll get over it, but I'll always remember him."

I wondered if anyone had told him that I would be winning the race the next day. I wasn't about to be the messenger of bad news. I'd had enough of that already. I just wanted to get safely through the next thirty-six hours, know the bad guys were rounded up, cuffed and stuffed in jail cells far away from me.

# 32

When I awakened on the morning of race day, it was obvious my sleep had been disturbed by bad dreams. My sheets were a tangled mess, and the way my hair stuck to my scalp, I'd been sweating heavily at some point during the night. Even my muscles were sore, as if I'd gone ten rounds with a nightmare.

Unnerved, I sat up fast and stared around the room, almost expecting to see chairs flipped upside down, broken lamps, or a shattered mirror. But everything was in place.

"For God's sake," I mumbled, "get a grip and get this day over with."

At ten, my driver whisked me from the hotel to Santa Anita, before dropping me off in the base camp. The guy had been driving me around for weeks and the only feature I knew well enough to recognize was the back of his head.

When I realized that he'd stopped in the exact spot where Dave had been sitting when a bullet smashed into his brain, a spiderlike chill crept down my spine. I jerked my head to stare at the roof of the food storage building. It was empty and I chided myself for being so skittish. Still, when I left the Lincoln Town Car, I made a wild dash for Pinky's trailer and darted through the door.

Inside her mobile office, the familiar rumble of the dryer, the scent of laundry detergent, and the colorful racks of designer clothing were comforting.

Since I'd last seen her, Pinky had touched up her roots with more pink and added a magenta stripe on one side. The lipstick she wore matched the stripe, and somehow, it all worked. She had my silks, white jockey pants and slender leather boots ready to go.

Grabbing the hanger with the clothes, and the cloth bag holding the boots, I made fast tracks for the silver trailer where Sally, the makeup artist, was waiting for me.

As usual, the thin woman with plain dark hair, who could transform my face and hair into Hollywood perfection, wore no makeup. She had me change into my movie wardrobe, sat me in a chair and put a plastic drape over my shoulders.

She studied my face a moment before setting out a tray filled with makeup. I stared at the tubes and pots that in her hands became magical potions.

After spritzing my hair with water, she sprayed mousse into her hands, worked it into my hair and blew it dry. Then she went to work on my face. I loved the results, but realized I would never be able to duplicate her talent. Like Jamie, it was fabulous, but not something I needed in my life.

Outside her trailer, I ignored the waiting limo, leery of being inside with my driver. Instead, I walked the few hundred yards to our barn's entrance.

In the stable yard, the extras were milling about in their shiny silks like a flock of exotic birds. Stan stood on the shedrow with Will, and I saw the unfamiliar faces of grooms that had been hired just for the day. I could tell Will was watching everything like a hawk. Since Reddinger and Millie would be filmed in the grandstand, they were the only missing characters from the movie.

The back of my neck prickled with the sensation of being watched. I turned to find the source. A very attractive woman, maybe a few years older than me, walked toward me. She wore silks, had extremely short, platinum-blond hair and wore two diamond studded rings in each of her ears. A tattoo of an eagle perched on her neck.

Moving next to me she smiled and spoke in a very low voice. "Hi, I'm Fia McKee, TRPB. You need to relax, okay?" Glancing at the extras and new grooms, she said, "We have a lot of undercover law enforcement here, so chill. You don't want to tip your hand."

"Okay. Thanks," I whispered. Something about her reminded me of my lost friend, Carla. Fia exuded the same confidence and self-possession.

Fia suddenly laughed and gave me a little shoulder punch like we'd shared a great joke. As she walked away, Jamie entered the stable yard and stared at her like he'd once stared at me, his eyes resembling heat seeking missiles.

Behind me, I heard Greta's voice. "He does like his women a little older, doesn't he? You're lucky to be rid of him."

"I know."

Ignoring Jamie, I panned the crowd, vainly trying to figure out who else might be undercover law enforcement. Probably better not to know.

When Gabriel and a man in black leather pants, a blue suede jacket and boots, stepped from Stan's office, the crowd grew silent. The two men moved to stand next to Stan and Will. Greta saw me looking, and whispered, "That's Zalaya's replacement from Estrella, Tommy John."

The guy was good looking in a Hollywood way, if perhaps a little too plastic. I noticed he was staring at Jamie, not bothering to hide his interest.

*Forget it Tommy Wommy, that boy is all male. Believe me, I know.*

With this thought, I felt the heat of a blush rise to my cheeks. Just because I wasn't heartbroken over Jamie didn't mean he couldn't still stir a response in me.

"Listen up, peeps," Gabriel called out. Gesturing at the newcomer, he said, "This is Tommy John, one of Estrella's directors. He's going to make sure we get everything right today and when we do, we're celebrating right here with champagne and catering, compliments of the studio."

We "peeps" smiled and a smattering of applause broke out.

Tommy John was still staring at Jamie, then his eyes moved to survey the crowd, before settling on me. "Darling, you're playing the role of Fay, am I right?

"Yes."

"Good, would you and Jamie hurry on up here and get your sheets and instructions for the race scene?"

Jamie and I nodded. As we walked toward Zalaya's replacement, he moved toward Stan's office and motioned us to follow. I thought Gabriel would come with us, but he gave Jamie a nervous glance and stayed on the shedrow. Will's eyes danced with amusement, and right then I knew no one had told Jamie he wasn't winning the race.

Inside the office, Tommy John sniffed disapprovingly and speaking to Jamie, he said, "I fear our trainer has a wee little problem with alcohol."

Jamie's reply was a noncommittal shrug, and I liked that he had no interest in gossip.

Tommy John handed us our sheets for dialog and a description of how the race was to play out.

We did a quick read through, and Jamie's mood soured instantly. "There's been a mistake!" he said, slapping the paper against his thigh. "This is ridiculous. I was supposed to win that race. It's in my contract!"

I took a step back and stared at the floor.

"You obviously neglected to peruse the fine print," Tommy John said. "There's a clause in there that says we have the right to change the overall script if circumstances deem it necessary."

Jamie, now in full Dillon mode, yelled at the director, "That's bullshit! Is this some sort of politically correct crap? You've deemed it 'necessary' to grovel before the Hollywood's demands to give everything away to women and minorities?" His anger fired at me. "Did you know about this?"

"News to me." I could lie with the best of them. The truth would serve no purpose. It would only add fuel to Jamie's flames. I was beginning to realize this race might be harder to "win" than I'd thought.

"We'll see about this!" He ripped the sheets in half, wadded them up and threw them on the floor before stalking out of the room.

"My, my," Tommy John said. "He does have a temper. Never mind, sweetheart," he said to me. "I was warned." He picked some papers off the desk. "I made extra copies. Would you mind giving these to him?"

"I think *you'd* better do that," I said, and left the office.

On my way to London Fog's stall, I realized I'd been too happy with Gabriel's news to question it. So, why did they want *me* to be the winner?

# 33

Santa Anita's Art Deco grandstand was painted the same soft green as the backside stables. Striped awnings decorated its walls, and gold racehorses, set in the Art-Deco style, glowed from its green walls. Combined with formal topiary standing at the base of the building, the grandstand provided a stunning backdrop to the racing paddock.

As Greta and I entered the oval enclosure, we moved past the camera of Gabriel's assistant which momentarily focused on the two of us before panning back to catch Jamie's entrance.

"Our handsome boy seems kind of pissed off this morning," Greta said. "What's up with that?"

Before I could answer, she said, "Wait, I know. It's because you're going to win the race, right?"

"Yup," I said. "He probably thinks it will diminish him in the eyes of his adoring fans."

"No, Nikki. It's more than that. I looked him up in the online tabloids. He's had, like, three girlfriends. They each lasted about a year and then he dumped them. You're the first one to dump *him*."

"Payback is hell," I said.

Greta grinned and said, "Apparently so."

I could only think of Jamie as *Dillon* today. He had neither looked at nor spoken to me since he'd stormed out of Stan's office. His anger was palpable and worrisome.

Maybe Jamie was showing his true self today. What if the Jamie I'd halfway fallen in love with was the act, and the real Jamie had a mean streak he'd kept hidden?

Forcing him out of my mind, I gazed outside the paddock, where towering palms and lush gardens were dominated by the spray and splash of the Kingsbury Fountain. Life-size statues of famous racehorses like Seabiscuit and Zenyatta dotted the garden, sending a prickle of awe down my neck. The sound of the fountain's water was soothing, while the imperious gaze of the statues was intimidating.

Jockeys and owners stood in the paddock with us as the horses paraded around the paddock's dirt path. A mob of extras, playing the role of excited fans, crowded the fence rail.

The canopy of blue sky above, the clear, eucalyptus scented air, and immensity of the grounds was something that could never be captured in a sound stage. For the first time, I was overwhelmed by the beauty and history of Santa Anita.

Art and life were crashing together, the coming race so real, a wave of dizziness washed through me. Shaking my head, I took a calming breath, my gaze seeking refuge in the horses.

Orlando had groomed London Fog's gray coat to a brilliant sheen, leaving his dapples looking like dark silver quarters. The horse knew exactly where he was and what was coming. His veins had popped and his muscles rippled. His neck arched as he pulled on the lead in Orlando's hands. It was all so real I was jolted with pre-race tension. I hadn't experienced it in a long time.

Since I was riding for Millie and Reddinger, I moved to stand beside them in the paddock. Gabriel moved in with his hand-held camera, as Millie wished me luck and Reddinger said, "Ride him like he was your own, kid."

I nodded and stepped back as they turned to speak to Jamie, who still refused to look at me.

"Riders up!"

The familiar call sent a surge of adrenaline through my veins. I stepped from the grassy center onto the dirt path as Rolando led London Fog toward me. Reddinger was suddenly at my side, making a cup with his hands as Rolando struggled to keep the excited horse from bolting. I thrust my knee into Reddinger's cupped hands and he lifted me into the saddle as London Fog continued moving forward. I gathered my reins, and my feet found the stirrups. Since we were in the three-hole, and Jamie was in the six, I'd mounted first. A quick glance back showed Jamie mounting Mystery Ride.

Rolando led us behind the first two horses along an L-shaped path that took us through a tunnel. We moved through it, and suddenly the race track was before us with a mob of fans crowding the railing. The winner's circle was to our left as we stepped onto the track, with the finish line directly across the dirt of the home stretch.

I glanced at the grandstand. The section near the finish line and the winner's circle was filled with extras. Big shots, dressed to kill, who could afford the best tickets. The rest of the grandstand was empty, but I knew Estrella would splice in NBC footage from the last Breeder's Cup to fill the stands for the conclusion of *The Final Furlong*, no doubt using the roar of the Breeder's Cup crowd as well.

As the two-horse was picked up by a pony boy and led away, a large buckskin pony was easing up to us. His rider was leaning forward to secure the lead strap through the bit's ring on London Fog's bridle. When the rider straightened, I was surprised to discover Fia McKee in the saddle. I was glad, too.

Rolando moved away, as Fia gave me a wink, and led us off before the grandstand at a jog.

Usually, the trainer would talk to the pony rider before the race and give brief instructions about warming the horse up. Sometimes the jockey gave those instructions if he knew the horse well enough. I didn't think Reddinger had spoken to Fia. Why would he, since how the race would unfold was predetermined?

Except Jamie was a loose cannon, and my horse was already on the muscle, his neck still arched, his ears pricked forward. He wasn't as fit as Mystery Ride, so I hoped he had more courage.

"Fia," I said, "don't do too much with him, just enough to loosen him up, okay?"

"You got it," she said.

Overhead, a news helicopter circled the track, adding yet another touch of reality.

The race would be run counter clockwise around the track, but at the moment we were moving clockwise toward the far turn where the horses would line up, then reverse to form the post parade before the grandstand.

Jamie and Mystery Ride cantered past us, and finally looking at me, he said, "Better get ready to lose, bitch!"

We weren't on camera yet, and his words were not an act. I'd always thought he was a professional, but his childish reaction to the change in the script told me otherwise. He was going to try and beat me.

Well, screw him. If I could, I would leave him in my dust. Now, my pre-race tension was the real thing. Though Gabriel could edit the film to make me look like the winner, that wasn't good enough. It was time for me to be a jockey again.

It felt like only seconds later that the post parade was over and we were approaching the starting gate. The gate crew walked forward grabbing the leather straps from the pony riders.

As Fia backed her buckskin away, she glanced at Jamie then back at me. "Good Luck. Looks like you'll need it."

I was too nervous to reply and my heart was jackhammering as I was led into the three-hole. The rest of the horses loaded, with only one resisting, causing two of the gate crew guys to join hands behind his butt, and push him forward until he gave in and entered his slot.

The long stretch of track loomed before us as I gathered my reins, grabbed a handful of dark gray mane, and grabbed the crossed reins with the other hand.

The track announcer yelled, "They're all in line!"

The bell rang as the gate crashed open. We exploded forward.

I had studied London Fog's past performances. He liked to lay mid-pack and come from behind with a quick turn of foot in the final furlongs, so I sat chilly, not urging him to the lead. We had nine furlongs, or a mile and an eighth ahead of us. I planned to cover him up and save him for the end.

It was a ten-horse field and a few seconds into the race London Fog and I were lying fifth, on the rail. It was a good position as long as we weren't boxed in later. Then I remembered I was in a movie and except for Jamie, everyone else was paid to make sure I won.

I continued to sit chilly on London Fog, happy to have him covered up by the first four horses, none of which were Mystery Ride. The almost black bay, Predator, was on the lead with the chestnut Gazelle lying in second.

Gabriel and his assistant raced behind us in the camera truck. Where was Dylan, anyway? I snuck a peek under my arm and saw him lying about seventh, but close on our tail.

As we raced down the backstretch, Jamie must have been asking Mystery Ride for speed, for moments later Mystery Ride's brown head appeared on the flank of Daisy Dan who ran next to me with Greta in the irons. Jamie drew even, then spurted ahead, pulled in front of us and slowed the pace ahead of Daisy Dan and London Fog.

"Watch it!" Greta shrieked. "You want us to clip heels?"

Both Greta and I had to stand in our stirrups to check the forward momentum of our horses before one of them struck the heels of Mystery Ride, an action that could cause a catastrophic spill on the track. Jamie glanced back with an evil grin.

Greta yelled at him. "You crazy son of a bitch, stop it!"

He laughed and surged forward, leaving Greta and me to collect our horses, and urge them back to racing speed. A chorus of curses sounded from the riders directly behind us, while others, who'd been safely off the rail, sped past us on the outside.

The field was entering the far turn and it would only be moments before we were at the top of the stretch. I was lying eighth, wondering if London Fog had enough late speed. This had to look like a horse race. I didn't want the other riders to pull their horses so I could pass. It would be too obvious, and God knows I didn't want to do this race over, not when London Fog was not that long out of knee surgery.

"Give us a hole, Greta," I cried.

She nodded, moving Daisy Dan away from the rail, giving us an opening to move forward and hopefully start picking off horses. London Fog saw the hole, and when I asked, he rocketed through it, moving away from the rail aiming for the center of the track. The pack of horses ahead of us were crowded three and four-wide on the rail.

We rounded out of the turn into the top of the stretch. London Fog, now well off the rail, saw the clear track ahead of him, switched leads, and blasted forward. Damn, this horse could run!

It was easy to pick off horses, especially with the help of the other riders, but Jamie was on the lead going all out on Mystery Ride, at least five lengths ahead.

"Yah!" I yelled at London Fog, not hitting him, simply showing him the rhythmical motion of the whip alongside his neck and shoulder. He found another gear, and four strides later, only Jamie lay ahead of us.

We were in the final furlongs and London Fog was grinding away at Mystery Ride's lead. Jamie looked back, saw us coming, and tried to get Mystery Ride to switch leads, find another gear, and reach the wire ahead of us.

Overhead the news helicopter tracked us. But the movie had turned into reality. This was a real horse race.

"Run you son of a bitch, run," I yelled at London Fog. I hit him once with the crop and damn if the horse didn't switch leads on his own, find yet another gear, and move head-to-head with Mystery Ride.

I didn't hit him again. He was giving me everything he had. *Please, God, don't let his knee give up. Not now!*

But London Fog would not be denied. His nostrils, and then his ears surged ahead of Mystery Ride's and we flew under the wire, the winners.

# 34

When we passed the wire, I stood in my stirrups letting London Fog gallop out at his own pace for a while before slowly reining him in, singing the words, "Easy, easy," almost like a lullaby.

Behind us, I saw Jamie jerk Mystery Ride out of his gallop, pulling the horse up, too quickly and harshly. Nice way to injure a horse's front legs.

I looked away, still easing London Fog until he was cantering. Just like in the real races, an outrider picked us up, and a woman with a microphone rode alongside us for an on-the-spot interview. Her camera held the NBC logo, another touch to make the scene more real.

We hadn't practiced for this scene, so, I just did what any excited winning jockey would do. Gasping for breath, I said, "He had a tremendous turn of foot in those last furlongs. Extra gears I didn't know existed!"

"How does it feel to win your first Santa Anita Derby?" the woman asked.

I squelched the snarky reply I felt like giving, and did what I'd seen so many top jockeys do. I started thanking Reddinger and Millie, for all their support and giving me such an excellent horse to ride, and so on and so on. Finally, the out rider pulled us down to a walk so we could turn and head back to the winner's circle, leaving the reporter behind.

As we broke back into a trot my body listened to the rhythm of London Fogs gait. He felt slightly off in the left front, where he'd had knee surgery. Thank God we were done.

When we neared the winner's circle, Reddinger and Orlando jogged onto the track and led the horse in. Millie ran up to my side, and we did a fist bump, before Reddinger lined us up for the win picture.

"Smile like you own the world," Gabriel's voice at my side. The rolling cart with the big camera was just outside.

It wasn't hard to smile, because I'd run a good race, and gotten as much out of my horse as Mike Smith could have. I was proud and happy.

Gabriel cried, "Cut! That's a wrap!" and around us everyone broke into applause, then started drifting away from the winner's circle. I heard the sound of rotors beating the air. For some reason, the news helicopter was landing in the infield. I'd never seen that happen before. But the copter was working for Estrella. Probably, they'd heard there was going to be a party.

I was ready to dismount, so glad it was finally over, when I noticed Tommy John standing below me with two men who'd just entered the winner's circle. One wore a gold necklace and one had a large diamond ring.

"Get off the horse," Tommy John said. "We need you to come with us to the sound stage."

*Screw that!*

Diamond's eyes bore into me, and a little smile played on his lips. It hit me like a sucker punch. He *had* seen me that day I hid in the recess of the staircase. I'd managed to convince myself he hadn't. I was wrong. Dead wrong, and the only witness to the murder of Zalaya.

"Get off the horse," Tommy John said again.

"Fuck no," I yelled. Where was all my protective law enforcement? No way I was waiting to find out. As I tried to boot London out of the paddock, Diamond grabbed my ankle, almost pulling me off the horse. Holding London's mane with one hand, I used the other to smack my crop across Diamond's eyes and the bridge of his nose. He howled with pain and let go.

But Gold Necklace had grabbed London's rein. The horse spun around him, a tight fast circle that almost unseated me. I could hear the engine of the copter. If these two men got me on the ground and forced me into that helicopter, I'd be gone before anyone realized what was happening. They'd escape, and I'd be dead.

Desperately, I held onto my handful of gray mane. I whipped Golden Ring's face, then smacked his windpipe with the crop as hard as I could. Choking, he let go of the rein. I booted London Fog out of the paddock and onto the track.

As I scanned left and right, trying to decide where to run, the two thugs made a beeline for the camera truck. They grabbed Gabriel's assistant, smacked his head with the butt of a pistol, dragged him out, and left him on the ground. The truck's engine roared to life and the pickup spun toward me.

I made my decision and headed to my right, away from the safety of the backstretch. Any path that led to the stables was wide enough for the camera truck to follow and overtake us. I aimed London Fog for the clubhouse turn, but kept him going straight, heading for the outside rail and parking lot beyond.

I was asking a lot of a tired, sore horse. I was asking him to flex that bad knee to the sharpest degree possible as he tucked his front legs to clear the rail. If he would even jump the rail. I felt guilty, terrified, and determined.

The rail was only a few strides ahead of us, the truck only a few yards behind when I heard the first pistol shot. It must have missed us. We were still flying toward the rail. London Fog did not slow, or try to prop and stop, he gathered himself, rose in the air and cleared the rail.

As we came down a hot, incredibly painful zing stabbed the back of my shoulder. I'd been hit. London landed awkwardly on the steep bank leading down to the parking lot. I lost my stirrups and fell, rolling down the bank and onto the pavement, the wind knocked out of me, the pain screaming in my shoulder.

More pain as the air came back into my lungs, but I was able to sit up and what I saw was terrifying. Diamond was standing on the other side of the rail, both hands holding his big pistol. He aimed the ugly thing right at me.

Nowhere to run, nowhere to hide, I waited for the final blast. Would I even hear it?

A shot rang out and Diamond collapsed forward onto the rail still holding the gun. Stunned, I looked up to see Fia on her buckskin holding some kind of shotgun. Diamond, though hit, still had his gun and tried to raise it once more. Fia blasted his head. It exploded into a red cloudburst that soaked my face and silks in a copper scented shower of blood and brain matter. *Like Dave.*

I rolled onto my knees and vomited onto the pavement, my whole body shaking, but my head jerked up. I was still afraid of Gold Necklace, but he was in the truck, streaking toward the infield and the helicopter, aiming to escape.

Fia slid off the buckskin, climbed the rail, and jogged down the bank to join me.

"You did good, kid," she said. "Real good."

An unmarked police car raced across the lot and stopped next to us. Detective Garcia and Diggs were up front, but Will was in the back. He flew out of the car and raced to my side.

"Watch it," Fia said, "she's been hit. Her shoulder."

"I can see that," he said, staring at the blood gushing down my arm and pooling at my feet. Will's hands were shaking as he gently grasped mine.

"We need an ambulance," Fia called to Garcia.

"It's on the way."

I felt so faint. I started crumpling toward the ground. Will caught me, gently lowering me the rest of the way.

My eyes searched for his. They were burning green, hot with emotion. I tried to smile, failed, and mumbled the words, "Thanks, Marshall."

The light dimmed to gray. My world receded into a black hole. Then there was nothing.

## 35

I was in the hospital for a few days. Will spent hours in my room, sitting with me. Greta and Gabriel stopped by, too. When Greta came, after asking about my wound, she griped about Jamie.

"I only saw him for a moment after the race. He didn't even ask what had happened to you, Nikki. When I tried to talk about it, he said he had a plane to catch, and walked away!"

"I think you finally met the real Jamie," I said.

"Yeah. What a bastard."

"Yep, a chapter I'm happy to close," I said

Agents Halchik and Thompkins dropped by to question me. Garcia also paid a visit. When I asked them what was going on with the cartel, they gave me the standard cop dodge, saying it was an ongoing investigation. I learned nothing.

When I was released and stepped outside the hospital, the California sun and fresh air drifting down from the Santa Gabriel Mountains reminded me how lucky I was to be alive. Will picked me up in his Durango, telling me we were expected at Detective Garcia's office.

My shoulder still hurt like a bitch, but the painkillers worked well enough. When I took them. Diamond's bullet had torn into the back of my shoulder, gone clean through, and exited out the front without leaving irreparable damage. But I was irritable, already sick of the bandages, the sling, the pain, and wasn't looking forward to weeks of physical therapy.

Most of all, I was frustrated by the lack of information from Garcia and the FBI, and said as much to Will.

"Look," he said, as we reached the civic buildings and park surrounding the police station, "I'm as anxious as you are to know what's going on. But even the TRPB is in the dark."

"Or at least they say they are," I said.

"That could be. But I think this meeting might be a debriefing for us."

"I hope so." There were so many unanswered questions. Like, if Estrella was working with the FBI at the end, why had they sent Tommy John, who had participated in my attempted murder?

Still, it was nice to park in the lot like normal people. Last time, I'd been dropped at the door, I'd dashed into the police station, terrified I'd be shot at any moment.

We entered the building to find Diggs waiting for us in the lobby. We took the elevator to the second floor, and Diggs led us back to the door of the same conference room we'd been in before.

Glancing at my wounded shoulder, he said, "You look like hell. Can I get you a Diet Coke?"

"Thanks for remembering," I said. "Yes, please."

Will opened the door to the conference room, and I was surprised to see five people already at the table. Special Agents Thompkins and Halchik were there along with Garcia who sat at the head of the table.

Fia McKee, her four-diamond ear-studs almost as bright as her electric blond hair, sat next to an older man. He had thinning hair that had once been red, but now was mostly gray. A whiff of his Old Spice cologne reached my nostrils along with the strong smell of fabric dye from the carpet.

"Nikki," Will said, "I think you know everyone here except Gunford Jameson. He's the head of the TRPB."

Interesting. Maybe I'd learn something today.

Will reached across the table to Jameson, "Hey Gunny, it's good to see you again."

"Likewise," he said. He lifted a pen from the table and twirled it in his fingers, staring at me.

'Nice to meet you, Ms. Latrelle. Hear you've been through a lot recently."

"Yes, sir. Thank you," I said.

Diggs came into the room and placed a Diet Coke at my elbow before sitting next to Garcia.

I was glad to have something to do with my hands, and spent some time opening the can and taking a few sips. Jameson was still twirling his pen. Maybe I should take that up.

"I want to thank everyone for coming," Garcia said. "For some of you, there are a lot of unanswered questions." He was gazing at Will and me as he said this.

"Agent Halchik has been asked to fill in some of the gaps." He made a gesture with his hand in Halchik's direction, and she nodded.

Looking at me, she said, "First I'd like to thank Nikki Latrelle for sticking it out, and allowing us to round up the Martinez Cartel in one neat package."

Confused, I asked, "How did that happen?"

"Both Lexo and Arjun Martinez got sloppy. They were here for the conclusion of *The Final Furlong.*"

"What?" Will asked. "They couldn't resist watching the culmination of their big money project?"

"Exactly," Halchik said. "The money laundering, of course, was important. But this was their first venture into Hollywood, and I think their better judgement got sprinkled with stardust."

"They came in that helicopter," she continued, "and when we stopped them from escaping, the pilot took a plea deal and revealed the location of their warehouse. We confiscated enough fentanyl and meth amphetamine to supply the entire West Coast. Cooperating agents in Panama were able to raid Lexo's home and confiscate computers with a lot of very interesting information about their international operations."

Halchick smiled. "We've sewn this case up so tight, *nobody* will get out. Except the helicopter pilot. He's disappeared into witness protection."

"So," I asked, "why did Estrella send Tommy John, if they were cooperating with you?"

"He probably got a better offer from the cartel, right?" Will asked.

"Exactly." Halchick replied. "These people can't help themselves. Money's their god and Tommy John's just another disciple."

"And Dave, the assistant cameraman," I said. "Was he trying to blackmail the cartel?"

"Yes, and that's why they killed him."

She kept talking, using a lot of legalese about their next steps, which I tuned out. I didn't care about all that, I just wanted to know it was over.

Thompkins and Garcia exchanged some last words, then all the law enforcement types thanked Will and me, said goodbye, and left the room. Only Jameson, Fia, Will and I were left. I looked at Will and started to rise from my chair.

"Sit down, Ms. Latrelle," Jameson said.

*Now what?*

"We've been talking," he said, glancing at Fia and Will. "You can ride, and you know how to handle yourself. We've recently had a position open for an undercover agent in the Thorough Racing Protection Bureau. I'd like to offer you that job."

Stunned, I felt my jaw drop. Embarrassed, I shut my mouth, then I glared at Will.

*You knew about this and didn't tell me?*

"Nikki," he said, "I think Mr. Jameson is waiting for a response."

I needed a job. I'd love to work in the same organization as Will. But a part of me was frightened. Did I want to be an agent, putting myself in danger? Mental images of Dave, Zalaya, Gold Necklace and their horrific ends floated through my head.

Across the table, Fia leaned forward. "I for one, would love to have you come on board."

Since Ravinski and Carla had died, I'd been like a ship lost on the ocean. Maybe the TRPB could become my home port. I pulled myself together and looked at Jameson

"I'm honored you'd ask me to be a part of your team, but I'll have to think about this." My words had been an automatic response based on fear and uncertainty. But in my heart, I knew I needed a place to drop anchor. I would take the job.

He nodded. "Take your time, Ms. Latrelle, take your time."

I turned to Will. "Have the *Final Furlong* horses been shipped out yet?"

"No, they're still here, until tomorrow. You want to go the barn and see them?"

"Yeah," I said. "Let's go now." I smiled at Mr. Jameson, and said, "It's where I do my best thinking."

We stepped outside the Arcadia PD, and climbed into the Durango. Will cranked the huge Viper engine hidden beneath the hood, and together, we headed for the barn and the horses.

Thank you for reading *Shooting Star.* I hope you enjoyed it! If you did . . .

1. Help others find this novel by writing a review on Amazon, Bookbub, or Goodreads. A fair and honest review is the best gift you can give an author!

2. My novels include The Nikki Latrelle, Fia McKee, and Quinn O'Neill mystery series. Want to know when a new novel is coming? Sign up for my newsletter here: https://www.sasscerhill.com/subscribe[1]

3. Visit my website for the latest news, appearances, and a glimpse of all my novels here: https://www.SasscerHill.com

4. Visit my Facebook page here: **https://www.facebook.com/SasscerHill**

My Bookbub page here: **https://www.bookbub.com/search/.?search=sasscer%20hill**

My Goodreads page here: **https://www.goodreads.com/search?q=Sasscer+Hill&qid=sS5ViRapb2**

And Amazon here: **https://www.amazon.com/Sasscer-Hill/e/B003LYXOMI?ref=sr_ntt_srch_lnk_1&qid=1617888371&sr=1-1**

---

1.      https://www.sasscerhill.com/subscribe?fbclid=IwAR0pOliHu_ib8t-WydRJfl7IsM2EHdXTEzqcJIL-itwmmPjQE923wQ7KBgzk

## Acknowledgements

A huge thanks to Jeffrey Buerstatte for his help and expertise in law enforcement and legal issues. Jeffrey is a former Undercover Narcotics Agent, Washington State; a former Special Agent and Agent in Charge, of the Bureau of Alcohol, Tobacco and Firearms, Portland, Oregon, Miami & Ft Lauderdale, FL; and a former Assistant U.S. Attorney, U.S. Attorney's Office, Southern District of Georgia. He still practices law in Brunswick, GA.

I also want to thank Karin DeFrancis of the Maryland Jockey Club for setting up my meeting with Pete Siberell, Director of Special Projects at Santa Anita Park. Because of them, Santa Anita rolled out the red carpet for me, wining and dining, while watching the races. Best of all, I was whisked away in a golf cart for a guided tour of the backstretch, where I met a lot of top-class horses and trainers, including John Shirreffs, the trainer of the legendary Zentatta. Shirreffs had a big bag of carrots in his shedrow and I had the honor of feeding a couple to Zenyatta's son Ziconic.

A thank you to Mike Vercillo, Community Affairs Officer at the Arcadia Police Department for answering my questions and offering guidance about the Arcadia PD.

My thanks for the savvy advice and encouragement from the wonderful writers of Misterio Press.

And finally, as always, huge thanks to my critique group, "The Assassins Guild." Couldn't have done it without you guys!

**Praise for the "Nikki Latrelle" Series**

". . . you'll be intrigued by Sasscer Hill's Racing from Death"– *The Washington Post*

". . smooth and vivid descriptive prose about racetrack characters and backstretch ambiance that reeks authenticity."– *John L. Breen, Ellery Queen's Mystery Magazine*

" . . . an utterly unique take on racetrack thrillers." - *Betty Webb, Mystery Scene Magazine*

"A page-turner, the book's sentences are short and crisp. The action comes off as authentic."- *Sandra McKee, Baltimore Sun*

". . a major new talent and the comparisons to Dick Francis are not hyperbole."—*Margaret Maron, New York Times Bestselling author and winner of the Edgar, Agatha, Anthony, and Macavity awards.*

"'Racing from Death' is an exciting thriller set in the world of horse racing, very much recommended."– *Carl Logan, Midwest Book Review*

**About Sasscer Hill**

Author Sasscer Hill was involved in horse racing as an amateur jockey and racehorse breeder for most of her life. Her mystery-thrillers portray the world of horse racing, and the skullduggery that big money and gambling so often attract. Her novels have won the Dr. Tony Ryan Best in Racing Literature Award (Flamingo Road) and the Carrie McCray Award (The Dark Side of Town). Her Nikki Latrelle books have also received multiple award nominations for Agatha, Macavity, Claymore, and an additional Dr. Tony Ryan Award.

Her recent novel, "Travels of Quinn" is a mystery-thriller based on the con artists known as Irish American Travelers.

Sasscer lives in Aiken, South Carolina horse country, with her husband, two dogs, and a cat.

Made in the USA
Middletown, DE
25 July 2021